MEXICAN SKIES

ALSO BY

J.B. HOGAN

TIN HOLLOW

FALLEN: A SHORT STORY COLLECTION

THE RUBICON: POETRY AND SHORT FICTION

LOSING COTTON

LIVING BEHIND TIME

ANGELS IN THE OZARKS

THE APOSTATE

MEXICAN SKIES

TWO NOVELLAS

J.B. HOGAN

STIRLING
OGHMA CREATIVE MEDIA
www.oghmacreative.com

ISBN: 978-1-63373-248-3

Interior Design by Casey W. Cowan
Editing by Gordon Bonnet

Stirling Press
Oghma Creative Media
Bentonville, Arkansas
www.oghmacreative.com

To all the friends I made during my times in Mexico.

Thanks to Casey Cowan for this incredible book cover and layout and to Gordon Bonnet for his highly skilled and professional editing.

MERIDIAN
SUN

1

Paige Warren sat cross-legged on the thick living room carpet looking through a box of old family photographs. She had the box wedged between her athletic legs and one end of an aging, off-white couch. When she finished checking out a photo she would drop it onto a growing pile near the edge of a long, low coffee table. At the other end of the couch, intently reading Raymond Chandler, sat her mother, Sherry. The strains of Mozart's 40th Symphony softly filled the otherwise quiet room.

Digging in the bottom of the photo box, Paige came up with several old pictures, gave them the once over, and started to drop them on the table, then paused. She looked at the pictures again, one at a time, looked over at her mother, then back to the pictures. She tilted her head to get a better angle on the pictures, her shining brown hair falling over one eye.

"Mom?" She held a photo up for her mother to see.

"Hmm?"

"Who is this?"

"Who's who, honey?"

"In this picture here."

Mrs. Warren glanced at the photo over the top of her reading glasses.

"It's your father, of course."

She paused in her reading long enough to look out a large window at the tranquil golden light cast by the late afternoon sun on their split-level townhouse and the nearby rock slabs known as the Flat Irons.

"I recognize Dad." Paige feigned exasperation. "I mean, who's this man with him?"

"Probably one of his employees, dear."

"Mother!"

Mrs. Warren reluctantly closed her book. The pages hit together with a little popping noise. She set the book down and stood up.

"For heaven's sakes. Let me see the darn thing."

"Ooh, darn thing. You're getting really rowdy there, Mom."

"Give me the photo."

Paige handed over the picture, then went back to the others she had dug from the box. Mrs. Warren took a quick look and set the photo face down on the coffee table.

"Well?"

"Well, what?"

"Aren't you going to tell me who he is?"

"Who who is?"

"Mother, what is the deal here? You're never secretive about anything. Who was this guy, an old flame? Competition for Daddy?"

"He was just a man who knew your father." Mrs. Warren smoothed out her skirt and looked away.

"Right, and the Pope's just another priest in fancy robes."

"Don't be sacrilegious."

"All of a sudden you're holding out on me. There's something up."

Mrs. Warren went to the living room window and looked out upon the darkening foothills behind Boulder. Paige retrieved the photo from the table and compared it to others she had taken from the box.

"There's nothing up, dear." Mrs. Warren didn't turn around.

"Uh-huh."

"Why do you care now anyway? We've had those pictures your whole life."

"I just saw them, that's all." Paige held up three photos, scrutinizing each carefully. "It looks like you were all good friends."

After a moment, Mrs. Warren turned and came over to see the photos. She sighed softly. Paige took her hand. Mrs. Warren squeezed Paige's hand, then stepped past her to sit back down on the couch. For a few moments they sat looking at each other.

"It's okay if we don't talk about it," Paige finally said.

"His name is Jack Dodge." Mrs. Warren reached over and lovingly ran a hand through her daughter's hair.

If Paige had been younger or if she had not been so surprised to hear that name, it might have sounded like her mother had said, "once upon a time." As it was, she sat up at wide-eyed attention, grabbed the photos and poured over them again.

"Jack Dodge? The Jack Dodge?"

"Well, he's Jack Dodge anyway, I don't know about 'the.'"

"You know what I mean, Mom, Jack Dodge the writer. The one who turned down the Pulitzer Prize and caused such a stink. The one nobody's heard of in years."

"That's Jack, all right."

Paige looked at the photos again. Besides the first one of Dodge and her father Tom Warren, there was another of the heavy-bearded Dodge standing between a young, relatively ordinary-looking Tom and Sherry. A third photo showed Mrs. Warren at her earth mother best, a leering Dodge leaning over her left shoulder.

"You guys must've been really good friends. This picture is just you and him. Tell me about him."

"There's not much to talk about anymore. It was a long time ago. We were young, we believed in ourselves, in our future. We were friends at school and then for a few more years after. We just sort of drifted apart eventually. Jack went off to do his writing thing."

"Writing thing! Mom, some of my teachers teach his books."

"I suppose they do."

"What became of him? Why did he leave it all behind?"

"Jack was impulsive. He was a wonderful young man in a lot of ways."

Paige studied her mother's face for a few moments, attempting to glean more than her words seem to say.

"Mom, you and Jack Dodge. You didn't." Mrs. Warren looked away. "After you and Daddy were married?"

"No!"

"But before?"

"We were young, Paige. Certain things weren't such a matter of life and death."

"Did Daddy know?"

"I don't know. I suppose. I… it's really none of your business. It's all been over for years."

"I'm sorry, Mom." Paige took her mother's hand. "I shouldn't be so nosy."

"There was a time," Mrs. Warren recalled, "when I thought Jack Dodge was the most incredible, romantic man I'd ever known. Strong, creative, free."

"But you chose Daddy instead."

"Yes. Tom was strong, too. In a different way. Solid, dependable. I guess I took the safe route. I don't regret it. I never will."

"Daddy was a lucky man."

Paige watched her mother's eyes as they sought a picture on the opposite wall showing Mrs. Warren and her late husband with a much younger, happily smiling Paige.

"Did I know Jack Dodge, Mom?"

"When you were a little girl, he used to come over still. He thought you were the prettiest child he'd ever seen."

"Wow, cool. You know, Mom, I heard he was last seen in Mexico. Steve Thompson and I are supposed to do our internships down there next month. Wouldn't that be great if I could find him? That could make my career as a reporter."

"Heaven forbid. I'm already worried to death about you going down there for their elections. If you go digging around for Jack Dodge, too, I'll be a nervous wreck the whole time you're gone."

"Oh, Mom, you told me you lived down there and that it was one of the best times of your life."

"I was with your father, and friends."

"Friends like Jack Dodge?"

"You may look a lot like me but you sure inherited your father's stubbornness."

"That's why I'm going to be a good journalist," Paige said confidently.

"I don't doubt it." Mrs. Warren walked into the kitchen and poured herself a cup of hot herbal tea from a pot sitting on a small electric stove. "Want some tea?" she called back to Paige.

"Do you still love him?" Paige stood up.

"Of course I do. Your father was a wonderful man."

"You know who I mean."

"Young lady." Mrs. Warren frowned at her as she came back into the living room. "Your imagination is running away with you. Jack Dodge was special all right, but he was also self-centered, moody, obstinate, and could be mean-spirited. That's who he was and probably still is, you'd be better off forgetting him just like I did."

"I will." Paige gave her mother a devilish look. "Just like you have."

Mrs. Warren sat down on the couch. Sipping her tea, she retrieved the Chandler novel and her reading glasses. Paige stood behind the coffee table watching her mother try to get back into the novel. Mrs. Warren finally looked up.

"Don't you have a story to get done for the paper, or something? You're taking up all my reading time with this nonsense about Jack Dodge."

Paige turned away from her mother who went back to trying to read. Mrs. Warren frequently glanced up from her book to see Paige continuing to study the photographs.

She walked over to the living room window and looked out at dusk spreading over town. Lights were coming on in the houses further on toward the Flat Irons which were nearly obscured now by the dark. A star or two had appeared high above, their twinkling filling her with the promise of excitement and adventure.

"Jack Dodge, huh." She breathed deeply. "Hmm."

Mrs. Warren might have heard that breath of youthful hope and anticipation but she didn't look up from her book.

2

Steve Thompson examined a series of photographs on the large monitor of an Apple PC in the Colorado University Journalism Department. He leaned back in his work chair to more carefully admire and evaluate them.

He was tall and lanky, with short sandy hair. In his blue jeans, long sleeve button-down shirt and ankle-high hiking boots, he could have passed for any young guy attending CU. Clean-shaven and square-jawed with intelligent eyes, he was good looking if not handsome, and what he might have lacked in appearance he made up for with a calm, personable manner.

He seldom got really fired up about any particular thing but today, as he carefully checked several pictures of a beautiful, fast-moving canyon creek, he felt unusually agitated.

He scrutinized the pictures from left to right. On the third and fourth pictures he saw what he was looking for—large objects apparently dropped alongside of and into the creek. In the fifth photo he saw a cluster of the barrels. He expanded the photo and checked it carefully. In it, he could plainly read *TOXIC WASTE* on the barrels. And in smaller letters, Front Range Chemical Disposal.

"Hot dog." He jumped and did a little celebratory dance. "Left themselves wide open. Yes, physical evidence. Nailed you, you rotten…."

He jumped around some more, doing phantom high fives with imaginary colleagues. Suddenly, in mid-step, his impromptu rejoicing was interrupted by a hard rapping on the door which was immediately followed by Paige Warren shooting into the room.

"Whoa, Paige. What the heck?"

"I got great news about the internship, you got time to go to the union?"

"Yeah, but look at these flicks. I got Front Range…."

"Come on. I've only got a half hour before lit class."

"But look." He pointed at the pictures on the PC monitor. Paige didn't see. She was already halfway out the door.

"You're not gonna believe what I found out," she said over her shoulder.

"But," Steve stammered.

Paige reached back and virtually pulled him through the door. He stumbled out after her.

—

It was a typical spring day in Boulder, the warm air made pleasant by a breeze, the deep blue sky dotted by infrequent, low lying cumulus clouds moving rapidly toward and dissipating over the plains that began on the eastern side of the Rocky Mountains. This was the Front Range, where the plains that stretch on to the Mississippi and beyond begin—a nearly unbroken chain of fields soon to be filled with the wheat and corn that would in turn fill stomachs, human and animal, all over the land.

Absorbed in their conversation, Steve and Paige took little notice of the beautiful day, nor thought of the plains and the sustenance it would provide. As they briskly walked toward the CU student union, Steve, still a little miffed and hurt by Paige's unconcern over his photo discovery, tried to down play the news she had broken to him.

"So he's an old writer who bailed out and disappeared," he said as they reached the door to the union, "what's the big deal? We're supposed to be going down there to report on the Mexican elections not on wasted, washed-up novelists."

"Yeah, but that's for school, don't you see, if we can locate Jack Dodge and interview him, it'll be front page news. National. Imagine no more boring interviews with college deans, no more digging up dirt on small time local yokels. We can do something really big time."

They found a table in the sparsely crowded union cafeteria, comically named after the supposed cannibal Alfred Packer, and sat down. Paige tossed her things on the seat beside her.

Across the table Steve thought about his pictures, the revelation they would be, the corruption they would expose, all of that submerged now in deference to her latest project that he always allowed to override his own.

He wondered why he could never say no to Paige and what it said about him, and her. If there was a him and her. Which he sometimes wished there was, but seldom deluded himself into actually believing. Either way, he had to show some character or, despite their friendship and her innate good qualities, she would dominate him.

"So what are the Mexican elections to you, chopped liver? Maybe there are a lot of things more important than this Dodge guy. Like the environment, for example. Where's your sense of commitment all of a sudden? Don't you care about stopping the people who are trashin' the planet anymore, even if they are just local yokels?"

"Of course I still care." Paige gave him a withering look. "But this is a special deal. Dodge might not even be in Mexico anymore, but think what it could mean if he is. And not just for me. Think what a picture of Jack Dodge would do for you. There hasn't been one printed in probably ten years. We're talking the cover of *Newsweek* here. With your name on the credit line. Picture that."

"That's your trip, you're the star here. The straight A triple major. Can't miss BWOC. You have an aura or something. Me, I'm content just to tag along. Your light is bright enough for the both of us."

"Steve, we've been friends a long time. You know I wouldn't go after something like this on a whim. This is an incredible opportunity."

He leaned back and sighed, letting the import of his own photographic work fade into the bright light that was her ambition.

"All right. How do we track this character? What do you want me to do?"

"I knew you'd come through, you're so dependable."

"Yeah, like a good dog."

Paige gave him a look that was somewhere between a smile of disapproval and a playful frown. He winced under its power.

"Okay, okay, I'll do it. Whatever you want. I'm your dog, uh, man."

3

Paige sat at a table in the CU library with a pile of books and magazines laid out before her. Dodge's record, it seemed, was decidedly not high tech. Among the books and magazines she had spread across the table were copies of his novels *Race of Iron* and *Time Corridors* as well as a copy of a national magazine with a somewhat clean looking, mature-appearing Dodge pictured on the cover. The caption read—*Jack Dodge: Neo-Hippie Guru or Burnt-out Cynic?* As she continued studying, Steve came out of the stacks to her left and stopped in front of the table.

"Hi." He held both hands behind his back.

"Hi." She was too engrossed in her reading to do more than glance up.

"Looks like you found a lot of stuff."

"Quite a bit, how 'bout you?"

"I might have something you'd find of interest."

"What?" She finally gave him her full attention. "What did you get? Something really good? Come on."

"Just a bunch of pictures and…."

"What?" She grabbed his sleeve.

"Ta-da!" He brought out an old video cassette from behind his back.

"You got a videotape of him? Wonderful. Where did you get it?" She picked up the unlabeled cassette and looked it over.

"I've got my connections, too, you know."

"Who?"

"Unnamed sources."

"How are we gonna play it?"

"I got a buddy who's still got an old VHS player. We can swing by and pick it up whenever."

"Cool, so… what's the tape got on it?"

"Huh, uh." He wagged his finger. "My surprise."

"Let's go." She immediately gathered her materials from the table. "And get that dinosaur VCR."

"We're on it," he said as they hurried from the library.

4

Steve lived in a large, cluttered studio that had once been a rear bedroom in a big white wood frame house in back of the area across Broadway from the CU campus known as "The Hill." The Hill area, which in fact was on a hill above downtown Boulder, had been populated in the 1960s and 70's by long-hairs, transients, and students who congregated in its cheap eateries, shops, and nearby neighborhoods to eat, smoke, and crash. Now it was mostly upscale stores and cafés reflecting the shift of Boulder from freak haven to yuppie paradise.

Steve's place was disorganized and cluttered with books, dirty clothes, and mostly empty food containers. In addition, littered about the place were signs of his profession-to-be—lenses, cameras, and more photographs than you might expect to see in the new digital age.

While he fiddled with his TV and VCR in preparation for showing the Jack Dodge video, Paige cleared a spot for herself on the arm of a small sofa and explained what her library research had uncovered.

"It's funny," she addressed Steve's back, "he put out four novels altogether and one book of short stories. The books were well received by the critics and he had a promising academic career going. Then he was awarded the Pulitzer Prize and bam, he turns it down, walks away from his job and takes off for Mexico, where, the magazines say, he had already spent a lot of time."

"Your folks were in Mexico with him, right?" Steve hooked a cable from the back of the VCR to the back of the TV.

"Yeah, back in the day. I'm not exactly sure when. Mom wasn't too specific. She seemed a little upset by his name popping back up after all this time."

"Oh, yeah?"

"Yeah. Are you about done with that or do you want me to fix it?"

"I got it." Steve stepped back and turned on the power to both the TV and VCR. "And so what was the book that won, you know, the one that he turned down the prize about?"

"That was *Time Corridors*. I skimmed it. Depressing. Death and trapped in time kind of stuff."

"This Dodge sounds like a major fun kind of guy."

"I wonder what really made him do it?" Paige tapped her chin with her right forefinger.

"Check out this tape," Steve told her, "I think you're going to like it. We'll play the whole thing, but first there are a couple of places I especially want you to see, right now."

"Excellent."

Paige noted immediately that on the tape Dodge did not appear to be a lot older than he had been in the pictures her mother had, and that he was about the same age as he had been on the magazine covers she'd seen at the CU library. His beard was short and well-trimmed and his hair was shorter with some gray emerging at the temples.

The interviewer, a Dick Cavett clone, adopted an attitude of engrossed sincerity toward his subject. Dodge himself seemed amiable enough, though perhaps a bit intense. While Paige catalogued her initial reactions to seeing Dodge, Steve advanced the tape to the spot he wanted her to see.

"This is the first part here. Check it out."

She gave him a thumbs up sign.

"Well, Jack," the interviewer said to the flickering image of Dodge, "I might as well jump in and ask the question everyone out there is going to want to know. Why did you do it? Why turn down the Pulitzer?"

"Why not?" Dodge said.

"How about the monetary award?" the interviewer continued. "The status? The opportunities it would mean for you? A place in literary history? I would say those are good reasons."

"I don't need the money." Dodge paused long enough to make the interviewer itchy and Paige appreciative. "I don't care about the status or the opportunities. And any place I might have in literary history will be determined long after I'm gone and hopefully will be decided by an evaluation of my work and not my sheer luck in being named for an award."

"Sheer luck?" The interviewer was incredulous. "Aren't you being a bit *too* humble, Mr. Dodge?"

"There's no such thing as being too humble, unless maybe you're talking about a Mexican *campesino*."

"Seriously," the interviewer pushed the conversation back to his main question, "why specifically did you decline the Pulitzer?"

"I am serious. Very much so. But to give you as specific a reason as I can, awards trap you, define you, limit you. The prize gets tacked on like an extra last name. Jack Dodge, Pulitzer Prize winner. You know?"

"Yes, I do know," the interviewer began, "and it sounds great, I…."

Steve jumped up and stopped the tape.

"Oh," Paige cried, "keep it going."

"Nah, it gets real dull." Steve turned down the volume on the TV. "Let's go to the next part I want you to see." He fast-forwarded the tape causing the interview to sail by like a film version of a 33 1/3 record played at 78 rpm.

"I thought it was fun."

"Check this out." Steve stopped the tape and started it again. "I think this is it." The speeding film halted, then kicked into regular forward speed again. He turned up the sound.

"My sources tell me," the interviewer was saying, "that you've been dividing your time between Arizona and Mexico…."

"Yeah, this is it," Steve said over the interviewer's voice.

"Shh," Paige hissed.

"...and more Mexico than Arizona. Is this a south of the border Hemingway in Paris thing or are you just doing a Kerouac-Cassady expatriate routine?"

"Actually, I never thought of it either way." Dodge looked a little put out by the question. "Though there is a little of both in it, I suppose."

"How's that?"

"Well." Dodge visibly forced himself to take the interview seriously. "The little *pueblo* where I like to stay has a considerable artist colony and I've been told Neal Cassady was found on the tracks outside of town."

"What's the name of the place?"

"San Miguel de Allende."

"Outstanding." Paige clapped her hands. "You're mine, Dodge."

"Oh, yes," the interviewer went on, "I've heard of it. That was where Cassady died. Despite that unfortunate incident, it does have sort of a romantic reputation, doesn't it? A place to go to get away from your troubles, a place to find yourself after a bad experience—like the breakup of a long-term relationship. Am I getting warm, Jack?"

"I don't know about warm, but whatever you're hinting at, I wouldn't tell you, anyway. It's too personal."

"So that's it, this is all about a woman, isn't it?"

"No comment."

"You won't give me a scoop?"

"The scoop you're getting is this interview."

"How's that?"

"You'll see in a few years," Dodge said cryptically.

The interviewer looked puzzled and there was a pause. Steve used the break to stop the tape.

"Well?"

"Unbelievable," Paige said. "We've got our lead. We've got an idea of his motives. Outstanding, Steve. I want to watch all of it."

"I'll rewind it."

Paige stood up and hugged him.

"I did good?"

"You did great."

Paige turned her 100-watt smile and most appreciative, disarming look on him. All Steve could do was shuffle a little and look down at his shoes. It was his only defense against her.

5

The little *pueblo* of San Miguel de Allende in the Mexican state of Guanajuato seemed lost in time. Its narrow cobblestone streets hinted at an older, perhaps simpler past, as did its colonial mansions and quaint shops. The *jardín*, or central plaza, with its finely manicured trees, sat in the shadow of the *Parróquia*, the greatest of its many cathedrals. Throughout the town, foreign expatriates, store owners, and locals mingled with *campesinos* selling wood from the backs of noisy burros just as they did a century and more before.

Discovered around mid-20th century by North American tourists, artists, students, retirees, and film makers, San Miguel evolved into at least two distinct societies. With so many foreigners in town, local Mexican culture was often virtually invisible. Despite this, the two worlds found a way to coexist and maintained a symbiotic, though occasionally distrustful, parallel existence. Many years on, North American retirees, the local shop keeps, and indigenous wood salesmen mingled on the rocky streets in relative harmony.

On a warm, sunny afternoon just weeks before the Presidential elections, the *jardín* was especially active. In addition to the usual complement of noisy vendors, gawking tourists, and semi-permanent *yanquis*, the plaza spilled over with people in town to attend a political rally for the Kennedyesque opposition presidential candidate, Rolando Serrano, a local product.

Near the *Parróquia*, streets were blocked off and the area littered with festive streamers, balloons, and signs that declared support for Serrano, the popular leader of a left of center coalition party and son of a highly revered former state governor.

Serrano was in the middle of a spirited campaign speech, during which he occasionally paused to wipe the sweat off his brow with a soaked handkerchief, a gesture not lost on the sun-baked audience. At each pause, a local stepped forward offering the candidate a drink of juice, tequila, or whatever they might have. When the populist Serrano took one of the offered drinks, the crowd roared its approval.

Away from the main crowd, two North American men had strategically positioned themselves beneath the shade of a symmetrically trimmed laurel tree. One of the men intently watched the proceedings while the other poured tequila from a hip pocket bottle into a cup of juice.

The man watching the speech was tall, scrawny, balding, and scraggly-bearded. Eccentric looking, even Ichabod Crane-ish. He constantly scribbled in a thick, worn notebook filled with clipped out newspaper articles.

The other man, shorter than his companion, had gray, thinning hair and a bit of middle-age spread around the stomach, and seemed considerably amused by the note taking of the tall man. He swigged from his drink and tried to be heard above the crowd noise.

"What you jotting down there, Bartleby?"

"Descriptions of all the plainclothes *Federales* checking out Serrano and the crowd." The tall man didn't look up.

"I don't see any *Federales*." The shorter man gave the crowd a quick scan.

"Tequila doesn't exactly heighten your awareness, Jack."

Responding to something in the candidate's speech, the crowd around the men cheered.

"You made this bull up, Ahab," Jack said, when the noise died down and

Serrano continued his speech. "There's nothing going on here but a standard BS campaign stop."

The tall man still focused on his scribbling. "For a man with such potential, Jack, it's sad how you've chosen to blind yourself."

"*Omoo*." Jack loaded up his drink with more tequila. "You're the weirdest dude I've ever known."

"And you're the most wasteful I've known. Besides, this Philip Roth-Herman Melville routine is wearing a little thin, don't you think?"

Jack took another drink. He listened momentarily to Serrano's speech then turned back to face the tall man.

"Where's all that doodling get you, Mr. Melville West?"

"I write only for myself," West said. "You had a gift."

"Let's go over to The Infiernito and see Emma," Jack said. "You can show us what you've written about me."

"Not till Rolando's finished. We owe him that. Besides, I only have clips of you when you were a writer. When you were Jack Dodge."

"I'm still Jack Dodge. I'm still a writer."

"Of bottle labels, maybe." West finally looked at Dodge.

"I need a real drink." Dodge said.

"Exactly my point."

"Hey, I'm writing still, aren't I? I just do it under another name, that's all."

"When did you last send something out?"

"The *New Populist* has new people. I'm afraid they'll blow my cover."

"Blow your cover? Why would you care? Nobody knows who you are anymore. You don't have a cover to blow or even need one. You've wasted your gift and let your time get away from you."

"You know, I ought to pop you one, you self-righteous freak. You don't know squat about me. You don't know why I'm down here or anything else about me."

Some people in the nearby crowd turned to look at the loud gringos.

"I don't, huh? Well, I do know two things about you. Why you're here, for example."

"Yeah, tell me, swami."

In his belligerent state, Dodge didn't notice one of the plainclothesmen West had warned about move up close to him. When he realized the man was actually right beside him, he acted haughty and glared. The barrel-chested, pot-bellied man looked back, his expression masked by dark sunglasses.

West eyed the new arrival nervously, but persisted. "One, you're suffering from despair and guilt from the good old failed-youth syndrome…."

"Bull."

"And, like two-thirds of the *gringos* down here, you're getting over somebody. Somebody that you, a complete idealist despite your cynical, tough guy image, loved intensely."

"Oh, for God's sake." Dodge gave West a little shove. "This is pure crap."

"Stop fighting." The plainclothesman immediately stepped between them. The crowd quickly encircled the men, watching the curious scene unfold.

"Buzz off," Dodge told the man.

"Jack," West interposed quickly, "'Shades' here is one of Mendoza's men. Cool it."

Shades was quickly joined by two other plainclothesmen, both built just like him, one of them sporting a nice, fairly new, three-inch scar above his right eyebrow, the other wearing an incongruous pork pie hat that made him look like a bad Mexican imitation of John Belushi. They surrounded Dodge.

"You better move on, mister," Shades threatened.

"We'll move on when Mr. Serrano finishes his speech, Shades," Dodge retorted. "We're friends of his. We want to hear him."

"You leave here, now," Scar said. "We don't care who is your friend."

Dodge was ready to smart off again when a loud cheer went up from the crowd. The plainclothesmen took advantage of the sound and general excitement to push West and Dodge back toward the edge of the *jardín*.

Shades swatted Dodge a couple of times around the head and shoulders and gave him a little kick. In the scuffle, West dropped his notebook and papers. He hurried to retrieve them but Pork Pie grabbed them up and handed them to Shades.

"What is this?"

"They're my notes. Give 'em here."

"We'll have them checked."

"You jerks, they're mine. They're private. Give...."

Scar grabbed West by the shirt collar and tossed him backward. Dodge, sobering up quickly, led his friend away.

"Those are mine," West repeated.

The plainclothesmen again advanced menacingly.

"Forget the damn things, Mel."

"Fascist bullies."

"Shut up."

"Get away from here, *putos,*" Scar said.

"If these papers are all right," Shades said. "You'll get them back."

"We're going," Dodge said. "No problem."

"No problem," Scar mimicked Dodge, to the amusement of Shades and Pork Pie.

Dodge and West slunk off, humiliated and intimidated. The sound of the plainclothesmen's laughter mingled with the roar of the crowd as Serranos's speech went on.

6

"Well, that's that," Steve told Paige and Mrs. Warren. "The bags are all checked through to Mexico City and the seat assignments are squared away. All we have to do now is go through security and board. We can relax."

"Relax?" Mrs. Warren said. "I'm not going to relax until both of you are back here, safe and sound."

"Oh, Mom."

"You've got everything you need?" Mrs. Warren ignored Paige. "Passports, student visas, travelers checks…."

"Yes, Mom. We're completely ready. We're not kids anymore, you know."

"Oh, yes, you are."

"When you were my age, Mother, you were driving around Mexico with two crazy men. We're just going for a six week internship. We'll be okay."

"You have my cell and work numbers." Mrs. Warren turned to Steve. "Call me any time. I'm making you responsible. She won't pay any attention to me. She's got it in her head she's off on some romantic quest for Jack Dodge the Great Lost American Novelist. Try to keep her sensible."

"I'll do my best, Mrs. Warren. But you know, once she gets an idea…."

"Just keep her out of trouble. You're a man, you can do that."

"I'll try."

"Oh, brother," Paige said. "You two."

"I just worry, honey. Please be careful."

Mrs. Warren hugged Steve, who then stood to the side looking embarrassed. It was hard to tell which made him more uncomfortable, the goodbye from Mrs. Warren or his new role as protector of the ebullient Paige. Mrs. Warren then hugged her daughter tightly. Looking over her mother's shoulder Paige winked at Steve.

"I'm going to miss you." Tears welled in Mrs. Warren's eyes.

"I'll be back soon." Paige pulled back from her mother.

"Bye, honey." Mrs. Warren looked away.

"Bye, Mom." Paige hugged her mother again, then followed Steve.

"Jack Dodge is a dangerous man, baby," Mrs. Warren called after her daughter. "Be careful."

"What?" Paige cupped an ear with her hand.

"Go on." Mrs. Warren waved. "Have fun. Mexico is great, you'll love it."

"I love you."

"I love you, too." Mrs. Warren tried to be heard above the noise of the busy Denver International airport.

With a flurry of final waves, Steve and Paige hustled away. Mrs. Warren tried to watch after them, even after they passed through security and disappeared beyond it.

7

Dying sunlight penetrated the dark interior of *El Infiernito,* streaking the little bar with golden, smoky beams. There were only a handful of patrons, including Dodge and West, scattered around the small dusky room.

Emma Duarte, the short, pretty owner of *El Infiernito* was behind the counter. Dodge sat on a barstool across from her. West was behind Dodge, scribbling as usual—this time on loose leaf papers he had spread all over a table. While Dodge pounded tequila, Emma opened a fresh bottle of Superior beer as a chaser and set it before him.

"I don't want to lose business, Jack," she told the bleary-eyed writer, "but that stuff's gonna kill you."

"Oh, please. Save me the sermon, babe," Dodge replied coarsely. "Death is a piece of shit."

"Life's what kills you," West piped up, "not death. It's what killed you."

"Go to hell." Dodge didn't turn around.

"You're already there."

Dodge flipped up the middle finger of his right hand.

West didn't see the gesture.

"What's with you two?" Emma said. "Why the squabbling?"

"We got rousted out in the *jardín* by some of Mendoza's thugs," West said.

"You went to the speech? You know better than that. You should mind your own business. Mexico is for Mexicans."

"I hate getting old," Dodge grumbled. "It makes you so cowardly."

"Which Mexico?" West grilled Emma. "The Mexico of Porfirio Diaz and General Huerta or the Mexico of Zapata and Cardenas?"

"Either way it's ours, not yours," she told him.

"From the Grito de Dolores to Santa Anna," West kept on, "from Cinco de Mayo to the massacre of '68."

"You were probably down here even then, you old reprobate." Dodge perked up. "They gunned 'em down like nothing."

"You're drunk," Emma said.

"I need to be."

"It won't help."

"I don't remember so well when I'm drunk."

"What's your problem today? Feeling more sorry for yourself than usual?"

Dodge reached over the bar and rubbed Emma's shoulder. Even drunk he could still appreciate how gracefully she had aged, especially for someone whose entire adult life had been spent in dingy bars like El Infiernito. She pushed his hand away.

"So caring," he sniffed.

"I don't like you when you're this drunk. You're mean."

"He's sick." West looked up and tapped his head with a long bony fore-finger. "Aqui, in the alma, the soul. He can't get over how his career flopped."

"Shut up, Mel," Dodge growled.

"He was somebody once, and he chose to become a nobody. That's what he can't live with."

"Mr. Know-it-all." Dodge slammed down a big shot of tequila. He didn't bother to chase it with beer.

"You let a woman and a couple of hurts scare you into anonymity."

"Go to hell."

"Shut up, both of you," Emma said. "You're just fighting because Mendoza's men frightened you. You're like little boys. Taking it out on each other."

"We're fighting because Herman Melville there doesn't know diddly squat about me or my life."

"You know why you hate yourself so much, Jack?" West said.

"Why, Mel?"

"Because you couldn't live up to your own image. Because you couldn't be perfect. Because you're like everybody else—human, flawed, cowardly. The great Jack Dodge couldn't be that. So he ran off to Mexico and became a rummy."

"I've had it with you, you *maricón*." Dodge spun on the barstool and headed for West.

He grabbed West by the shirt and the two men struggled ineffectually, neither really hitting the other, until Emma hurried from behind the bar and separated them. Dodge, barely able to keep his balance, took a wild parting swing that easily missed West by feet and then fell in a heap over a chair, nearly passed out from the exertion. Emma and West lifted him to his feet.

"Help me drag him upstairs." Emma warded off a couple of drinkers who had started to move toward the scuffle.

With Emma on one side and West on the other, Dodge suddenly became tranquil and let his arms flop over their shoulders. They hauled him toward the back of the room where a set of stairs led to Emma's second floor apartment above the bar. They struggled to get Dodge up the stairs.

"I don't know why you put up with this character, Emma."

"It was different before. You remember."

"I guess. But look at him now."

"He was special once. He treated me good. I don't forget that."

"You're either a saint, Emma, or a fool."

"Let's just get him to bed."

"Okay."

West lifted Dodge's legs onto the bed. Emma took his shoes off and began to undress him. West headed back downstairs to the bar.

8

"Goodness." Paige took in the immense panorama of Mexico City from her window seat as the plane made its final approach into the airport. "Look at that."

"It's massive." Steve leaned over to get a better view. "Look at all the lights."

"Maybe Jack Dodge is down there somewhere," Paige said.

"Maybe he's not even in the country anymore."

"He's here somewhere. I can feel it."

"Great." Steve sighed.

Enthralled by the sight of the city, Paige hardly noticed Steve's reaction. She watched the buildings getting closer and closer until they landed smoothly and safely. The airliner had barely come to a stop and shut its engines down before she was up pushing Steve to get their things and get off the plane.

They cleared customs without a hitch and with a couple of skycaps towing their bags entered the bustling waiting area of the airport. Looking over the crowd, Steve spotted a thirtyish North American woman in a pair of stone-washed Levis and a light blue blouse holding up a sign with *WARREN* printed on it.

"There, Paige, there's a woman to meet us."

"Yeah, I see her, the school said the *Times* would send somebody out. Don't mention our Jack Dodge thing."

"Our Jack Dodge thing?" Steve furrowed his brow. Paige ignored him—as was depressingly usual—and waved to the approaching woman, who came up to them smiling broadly.

"Paige? Steve?"

"That's us," Paige said.

"Wonderful. Welcome to Mexico City. I'm Jean Holland."

Jean offered her hand, which Paige and Steve shook in turn.

"Thanks for coming to get us."

Jean looked to be in her mid-thirties, good-looking, with brown eyes, a fine nose, and full lips that frequently and easily formed into a radiant smile.

"No problem." She rubbed her neck below her stylish brown hair. "The city can be a little intimidating at first."

"I can see that," Steve said.

"It looks exciting to me," Paige said.

"That's one of the things it is." Jean's eyes crinkled.

"No doubt." Steve said.

"Well, I'm sure you guys would like to get settled in. Let's get a taxi and I'll take you to your hotel."

"I'm ready to start now," Paige said. "I'm not tired at all."

"Enthusiasm, that's good. But I am tired. I put in a full day already. So I'll just drop you two off tonight. The hotel has a restaurant and a bar if you're hungry or would like something to drink."

"You'll be by tomorrow?" Steve said.

"I'd planned to come by for breakfast if that's okay. I can fill you in on the details of the internship then and give you your press credentials."

"That'd be great," Steve said. "I know you can tell us and show us a lot we don't know."

"Sure." Paige noticed that Steve seemed to be taking a quick interest in Jean. "That'd be fine."

"This way." Jean pointed toward the far end of the airport. "I've already bought tickets for the taxi so all you have to do is hop in and go."

"What time will you come by in the morning?" Steve again got a look from Paige.

"How about ten? Too early? Late?"

"Nine-thirty?" Steve suggested.

"Nine-thirty's good."

The skycaps loaded the bags in the trunk of the taxi. Jean tipped them and chatted with the cabbie in Spanish as Paige and Steve climbed into the back seat. Steve mouthed "thank you" through the window. Jean waved. The taxi pulled away and roared off into the Mexico City night.

9

An early morning ray of sunlight shone through a bedroom window onto the face of Emma Duarte, waking her from a light sleep. She rolled lazily over to the empty side of the bed, flopping her arm on top of the tossed-back covers. She yawned and stretched and heard the shower being turned off, and then a low rumbling coming from the adjacent bathroom.

Propping two pillows up behind her, Emma reached for a cigarette out of a pack on a nightstand and lit one. There was more noise from the bathroom and then Jack Dodge came out drying his scraggly hair with a towel.

"You need a haircut." Emma exhaled smoke into the beams of sunlight.

"I suppose it is getting a little long."

"How do you feel?"

"Like the fool that I am, of course. Was I really bad?"

"No, you were good—for a zombie."

"I didn't mean that. Was I really, really bad to Mel?"

Dodge sat on the bed. Emma continued to smoke, but put her free hand on his leg.

"You were both frightened," she said softly. "Mendoza's men are animals. Running into them would cause anybody to act badly. But you should apologize to Mel."

"He really digs at me sometimes."

"Only because he idolizes you. You're everything he wishes he could be. You're the writer, he can only take notes."

"*Was* a writer. Past tense."

"You'll be one again, if it's meant to be."

"I'm sorry if I was mean to you."

"You're not so mean. Just unhappy."

Dodge stood and put on pants and a shirt that Emma had folded neatly the night before and set on a chair by the bed.

"I'm going down to *El Puente* to have breakfast," he told her. "Mel will be there. Will you come?"

"No, I'm going to see my sister in Guanajuato today. Go ahead."

"I don't know why you put up with me, Emma."

"That's what Mel said."

"No doubt." Dodge ran his hand through his hair and then walked to the door. "Thank you."

"For what?"

"For always helping me."

"*Para servirle, Señor* Dodge."

Dodge essayed a weak smile at Emma's playful formality, then with a little wave left the apartment. She stared at the closed door for a moment, sighed deeply, then stubbed out her cigarette and got out of bed.

10

Jean Holland joined Paige and Steve for breakfast in the top floor restaurant of the Majestic Hotel. The hotel was housed in an older, nondescript building at the edge of Mexico City's jewelry store district, which emptied out into the *zocalo*, the city's main plaza. Its interior was clean and neat, reflecting its mid-to-up-scale clientele. There was a large inside courtyard, the floor of which was made of Spanish tile, which rose up unblocked except for light, plastic skylights on the occasional floor, from the main lobby to the roof of the building.

"So, how are we doing this morning?" Jean said, while a small army of waiters scurried back and forth serving the crowded restaurant.

"Excellent food." Steve wolfed down a breakfast of scrambled eggs, bacon and wheat toast, with an orange juice chaser. "This is a nice hotel."

"Didn't they film *Missing* here?" Paige savored an order of spicy *chilaquiles.*

"Is that the film with Jack Lemmon?"

"Yes."

"I'm not sure," Jean admitted, "but I think it might have been around the corner at El Gran Hotel."

"I saw that movie once," Steve said. "It was good."

"So," Jean said, "how's you guys' Spanish?"

"I had four years in college," Paige answered.

"She's got a triple major in English, Journalism, and Spanish," Steve added helpfully.

"Yes, I read that in your file. But how about actual speaking?"

"I think I'll do okay," Paige said confidently.

"All right." Jean turned to Steve. "How about you? Are you a triple major, too?"

"Uh, no, I'm just a dumb photographer." He chuckled. "I do know *leche* and *pan tostado*, though."

"Well, that's a start." Jean said. "Anyway, we have a good deal for both of you. First on the agenda, before you begin the actual internship, you'll have a nice week of total immersion at a private language school in Cuernavaca. It's a new program this year and we think it will improve the quality of the experience for everyone involved."

"Sounds great to me." Steve took another piece of toast from a stack in the center of the table. Jean offered him a bowl of jelly which he turned down.

"Exactly what is our assignment?" Paige pushed away her mostly empty plate. "I mean, besides covering the elections in general."

"Specifically," Jean explained, "we would like for you to cover the Serrano camp."

"He's the opposition to PRI and PAN?"

"Yes. I see you've done some homework, Paige."

"Some."

"Well then, you probably know that Serrano is 'the' primary opposition to the two larger parties. He's the leader of a coalition of center-left parties united to try and defeat PRI and PAN. PAN, you may know, is basically the conservative party. They've been around a while but have only gained traction in the last several elections. PRI, of course, was formed after the Mexican revolution early in the 20th century and won every presidential election until Vicente Fox of PAN broke their long string. Your man Serrano's father was a great, left-leaning leader of the 1930s and the son seems to be the best chance in a long time that the liberal-left has had of winning the presidency."

"Sounds great." Steve finished his breakfast, wiped his mouth and hands with a napkin and settled back in his chair. "What do we do?"

"We want you two to put together background material on Serrano and the coalition—history, connections, leaders, with lots of photos. This can be more than just an internship. There'll be a lot of international interest in the elections, so your stories might have a shot at being picked up by the wire services and by papers all over Mexico, Latin America, the U.S. and even Europe."

"Excellent," Paige said, "that's what we want. Will we work out of here, I mean Mexico City?"

"No, Serrano's based in San Miguel de Allende, his hometown, a little village north of here." Steve and Paige exchanged rapid glances and he caught his breath at the excitement in her eyes. "There are only a few weeks left in the campaign, so Serrano will be on the move a lot, but he always returns to San Miguel. He's much the populist leader, like his father."

"I'm ready to go right now," Paige asserted.

"Let's let our breakfast settle first."

"Will you be going with us?" Steve said hopefully.

"No, your point man, Andres, will drive you over to Cuernavaca later today and get you set up at the school. Next weekend he'll come back for you and take you to San Miguel. San Miguel's also his home, so he's looking forward to getting to work there for a while. He knows the ropes, so don't hesitate to ask him anything. He's a great resource."

"Sounds terrific," Paige said, "you've really got it planned out."

"A few years ago one of our interns got—well, a little out of control."

"What happened to him?" Steve said.

"Her, she, it was a girl, got involved with one of the men she was covering, a well-known lawyer, got herself in the family way and didn't want to go home, et cetera, et cetera." Steve tried to give Paige a knowing look, but she refused to pay any attention to him. "Since then we try to keep a little better eye on our interns. I'm sure we won't have that problem with you guys, you seem too level-headed."

"Level-headed. That's us all right. No problem."

"Right," Steve said, his words and tone lost on Jean but not on Paige, "we wouldn't do anything as irrational as that, huh, Paige?" She gave him a dagger-filled look.

"No, Steve," she said icily, "of course we wouldn't."

"Great. Then we're all squared away."

She lifted her orange juice glass for a toast. Paige and Steve did as well.

"Welcome to Mexico, *salud.*"

"*Salud,*" Paige repeated.

"Cheers," Steve said.

11

Jack Dodge breakfasted as usual at *El Puente* restaurant located on an extremely narrow cobblestone street behind San Miguel's main church, the *Parroquia*, a little over a block from the *jardín*. *El Puente* doubled as a full-service mail, phone, fax and wi-fi service center for the colony of North Americans populating San Miguel in varying numbers throughout the year. The mail was being handled, as it almost always was at this time of day, by amiable, long-time San Miguel resident Martha Price. Dodge went directly up to the service counter to inquire about his mail—or lack of it.

"Hello, Martha, anything for me?"

"Morning, Jackie, let me check." She leaned back and checked his mail box, number 33, which was in the center left of a wall of small open mail slots. "Sorry, nothing."

"Sure it didn't get mixed up with old man Hornsby's there in 23 by any chance?" Dodge noted the extremely full mail slot directly above his own. Martha thumbed through the pile of mail in 23.

"Nope, nothing there, either. You'll just have to write somebody or write another famous book if you expect to get any mail. Or maybe try to come into the modern age and, God forbid, get a computer and the internet."

"Right, fat chance of that. They put fresh coffee on in the restaurant lately?"

"I believe so. Smells like it anyway."

"Excellent. Keep an eye out for my mail, okay?"

"Expecting something special?"

"I don't know. Just haven't had anything for a while."

"I'll watch for you. Have a good breakfast."

"Thanks."

Dodge left the service counter and walked a few steps into the building down into an open area that housed a small restaurant. There were six small tables in the room which was decorated with innumerable, healthy plants and a few bird cages from one of which a parrot squawked out at irregular intervals a surrealistic version of the Flintstones theme. The place was moderately busy but he easily found Mel West sitting alone at one of the tables, writing, as usual. Dodge approached his friend with some trepidation.

"Can I join you? I wouldn't blame you...."

"Sit," West said bluntly. Dodge pulled up a chair directly across from his friend. "You look a little rocky."

"I've been better."

"Uh-huh."

Dodge looked around the room at the handful of local regulars breakfasting at El Puente. A young waitress appeared at his side.

"Do you want to eat this morning, Mr. Dodge?"

"*Sí, pero solamente pan tostado y cafe—bien calentado y negro*. Just toast and coffee, hot and black."

"*Muy bien*."

When the waitress had gone, Dodge turned his attention back to West, though he was reluctant to make eye contact with him.

"Mel, I don't know what...."

"Save it, Jack."

"But I said really stupid things. I hurt your feelings, I'm sorry."

"Don't flatter yourself, Jack. I know you too well. If I paid attention to what you said when you were drunk, I'd be stupider than you are."

The waitress returned with a cup of coffee which he pursued with immediate intensity. While he was drinking, an older North American artist, Bruce, stopped by the table.

"Coming to the poetry reading at the Institute tonight, gentlemen?"

"Maybe so." Dodge savored the aroma of his coffee.

"How about you, Mel?"

"Unlikely."

"Well, if you change your mind or minds." Bruce began to move away. "You're both welcome." He went on to a table further back in the room.

"You want to go to that later?" Dodge said.

"No, and don't patronize me. I said I'm not pissed about last night, but I don't feel like going to a useless poetry reading with you. Besides, you should be crawling back to Emma, not me."

"They're not such bad folks, really, you know." Dodge ignored West's remarks, referring to Bruce and his artist friends.

West looked at Dodge's tired, bloodshot eyes. "You know, I think I like you better drunk. When you're sober, you get so contrite."

"I have reason to be. I'm basically a screw up."

"No deal, Jack, I'm not buying into any of this. Just forget it. Nothing's lost. We go on like we always have."

"I'm sorry Mendoza's jerks took your notebook."

"So am I."

"You going to try to get it back? We could go see Rolando."

"No, forget it. It wasn't important. I don't know. Well—maybe. Don't worry about it."

"You're not an easy man to get forgiveness from, Mel. I'm trying to apologize, damn it."

"If I forgive you, will you go bother somebody else?"

"Promise." Dodge put a hand over his heart.

"You're forgiven." West crossed himself. "Now please go back home and grovel for Emma, or pawn yourself off on some other poor schmuck. Brucie and his little clique over there, for example."

The waitress reappeared with Dodge's order of toast and a coffee refill. He chuckled and stood up with his meal.

"Okay, pal, I'm going. It's serious literary discussion time."

"Very good." West concentrated on his note taking.

"See you later at Emma's?"

"Life never changes for the gringos in San Miguel, that's why we stay here."

"I'll take that as a yes."

"Take it as you please."

Satisfied he had made peace, Dodge walked over to Bruce and his group. They welcomed him with laughter and jokes and made room for him at their table. West glanced over once, then lowered his head and went back to writing.

12

The road up and over the mountains from Mexico City was not especially crowded. Paige and Steve absorbed the sights and smells of the Mexican countryside while being driven to their language school in Cuernavaca by Andres, the point man for their internship. Behind them Mexico City was almost lost in its usual thick layer of smog, but on either side of the road were sub-tropical fields and small villages. The spaces in between were dotted by colorful and, even from the car, wonderful-smelling food stands that sometimes threatened to spill right out onto the highway.

Because Andres hailed from San Miguel, like the politician Serrano, Steve in the front seat and Paige from the back pumped him for information as they traveled. Steve tried to keep them focused on the internship in order to avoid Paige's line of questioning, that he expected would inevitably turn to the obscure object of her intense interest.

"So Serrano's really a man of the people, huh, Andres?" Steve said, as they passed a group of wood-laden burros kept in line by an old *campesino*.

"Yes," Andres answered simply.

"His father was a great nationalist leader, no?" Paige said.

"Yes, in the 30s, with Lazaro Cardenas."

"Was Cardenas the greatest Mexican president?" Steve wondered.

"Along with Benito Juarez, *sí.* Many people still believe so. Cardenas was a great man. A real man of the *campesino* and the *obrero*."

"What does that mean, *obrero*?" Steve said.

Paige answered for Andres. "It means worker."

"That's right." Andres' friendly face was framed in the rear view mirror. "You speak Spanish already, *señorita*?"

"Some."

For a few moments it was quiet in the car as they passed a small town with many food kiosks right at the edge of the highway.

"Andres, can I ask you a question about San Miguel de Allende?"

"Of course."

"Do you know if there's a writer there named Jack Dodge, a *gringo*?"

"I don't know, *señorita*, I left San Miguel some years ago and now I only go back to visit my family for the holidays. But there are many writers there, and *artistas*. What does this Jack Dodge look like?"

"By now he's older than you might have seen him. Wait, I have a picture." She dug the photo of Dodge and her mother out of her bag and handed it to Andres. He glanced at it a couple of times then handed it back. "What do you think?"

"Maybe, he looks familiar. Some years ago there was an Americano writer who came to San Miguel. He was famous, but wild."

"That's him." Paige nearly squealed with excitement. "That's him, Steve. I knew it."

"Incredible," Steve deadpanned, "major breakthrough."

"I knew I'd find him."

"I hate to be a downer, Paige, but the fact that Andres might think it was Dodge years ago isn't exactly evidence he's there now."

"That's right, miss. It was a long time ago."

"Listen to the man."

"Nope, I've got a feeling about it. For whatever reason, he's still there all right. Somehow he just got lost. But he won't be lost much longer."

Steve exhaled and turned again to the window. Paige settled into the back seat with a satisfied smile. Andres drove on silently. Ahead, in the distance, Popocatepetl rose majestically above the Mexican terrain.

13

About ten-fifteen in the morning, chunky, middle-aged Connie Miller relieved Martha Price behind the *El Puente* service counter. The day's stack of mail from the Mexican post office sat on the counter wrapped in a big rubber band. Martha scurried about getting ready to leave. Connie took the rubber band off the mail and, peering through her thick bifocals, thumbed through it.

"I'm sorry to leave you in the lurch like this, Connie, but I've got to get to the doctor's office this morning or I'll never get my new glasses."

"It's okay, hon, go ahead. I understand. I'm blind without mine. I can handle it here. Folks'll just have to wait a few minutes longer than usual is all. It'll help break up their routine."

"Sure you don't mind?" Martha came out from behind the counter and walked toward the front door.

"Go on," Connie assured her, "hurry. You've been complaining about your eyes since I've known you. Scoot."

"Be back in a little while."

"Okay, kid."

When Martha had gone, Connie sorted the mail in earnest, placing each piece in the slots on the wall behind the counter. After she had done several, she paused and held one up.

"For Jack Dodge from somebody Warren in Colorado. Maybe this is the one Martha told me he's been looking for."

Connie placed it into the crammed box number 23, directly above Dodge's box number 33 and went on sorting the mail, whistling as she worked.

14

Cuernavaca was once to the south of Mexico City what San Miguel de Allende became to its north—a quaint hillside *pueblo* that drew foreign artists and students like a magnet to enjoy its tranquil, picturesque atmosphere. In the distant days of the 16th century, it had been one of the homes of the conquistador Hernan Cortez, and two centuries later served as the same for Emperor Maximilian during the French intervention. In the second decade of the twentieth century it had been a crucial center in the agrarian revolt led by perhaps the greatest of all Mexican heroes, Emiliano Zapata.

Over time, however, Cuernavaca had grown to be a virtual extension of Mexico City, whose residents—known by the mildly pejorative term "chilangos"—practically overran it every weekend. Even without that flux, it had evolved into a loud, overcrowded town whose narrow streets were gorged with cars and roaring, clanging buses. Yet for all the newfound urbanity—both good and bad—Cuernavaca remained a beautiful town with a climate that gave it a feel of "eternal spring," just as the travel brochures insisted.

Like most Mexican towns, Cuernavaca's central plaza, or *zocalo*, with its tree-lined *jardín*, served as the social hub. Several open-air restaurants around the outside of the plaza were typically filled with locals, tourists, and students engaging in a favorite pastime—people watching. The area stirred late afternoons when the sun cast a gentle, fading light on the fully leafed tops of the trees. Locals, mostly couples—young and old—were joined by groups of ubiquitous college kids from Cuernavaca's many language schools enjoying a beer and sandwich or snack at one of the many cafes.

Steve and Paige's language school was located in a hilly middle class neighborhood about a mile from downtown. Like so many businesses and homes in Mexico, the school was blocked off from the street and world by large buff-colored adobe walls. And like so many of those other structures, when you got past the walls it became a miniature tropical paradise.

The school consisted of a half dozen buildings bustling with foreign students mostly from the U.S. Beneath the welcome shade of well-trimmed palms and almond trees and among the clean and precisely-pruned beds of geraniums and orchids there was a small snack bar, a library, and two pools—one just down from the snack bar and one in back of the complex, where the dark green carpet of manicured grass was least trod upon and most thick.

"I love it here." Steve set a Sidral orange soda on a table and pulled up a white metal chair beside Paige in the front patio area. "It's like a small college campus, only more beautiful. It's incredible that the *Times* paid for the week here. I could stay for weeks, months."

"It's okay," Paige responded unenthusiastically. "I'm sure they got their money from the contract with CU. It isn't a freebie."

"Whatever, it's a great place and a good deal. I'd like to study for a whole month at least, instead of just this one week. I'd really start getting the hang of Spanish by then."

"You can't learn it by just studying in a school. You have to get out into the culture, interact with the people."

"We've only been here a couple of days."

"Besides, Jean Holland is in Mexico City, not here. I thought you thought she was so neat."

"She was really nice, pretty, too."

"Steve Thompson," Paige said, "she's a professional woman. She wouldn't be interested in a kid like you. Besides, she's too old for you."

"What's the matter with you? All I said was that she was nice. And where do you get off calling me a kid? Jean's not that much older than we are."

"I just don't want you getting hurt. Remember her warning about the girl intern who got out of control down here."

"For crying out loud, of all the people to warn somebody about being out of control. All you want to do is chase after this stupid Jack Dodge and he's twice your age at least."

"You don't get it, do you, Steve? Dodge is our ticket to the big time. Fast. He's going to make stars of us both."

"What a load."

"Don't shout."

"I'm not shouting," he nearly shouted. "You're just playing a game here. If you ask me, you're already sweet on this guy and he's nothing but an old drunk, a washed up has been. Don't tell me who's in control and who isn't."

Paige looked away sullenly. At the sound of a bell indicating the beginning of the next hour of classes, Steve grabbed his book bag and stood up.

"I'm going to class because I like it here and I intend to learn something."

He walked off toward the administration building and on to the classrooms at the back of the complex. Suddenly Paige jumped up and ran after him. She caught him at the steps leading up to his class.

"Steve." She grabbed his book bag. "Wait." He turned toward her, annoyed. "I'm sorry. I'm just being grumpy. I don't know what's the matter with me. I'm anxious to get on with it down here. Forgive me?"

"I'll see you later." He pulled away. "I have to go to class."

"Steve. Steve."

"Later," he said over his left shoulder, "not now."

"Damn."

Paige turned around on the steps and nearly bumped into a group of students heading for class. She slipped by them, ignoring their stares, and headed back to the snack bar.

—

On Thursday evening of their week in Cuernavaca, Steve sat by himself at a small table toward the back of the open air *La Primavera* Bar, which fronted the Cuernavaca *zocalo*. He was drinking a beer and watching the parade of humanity pass by. At a far end of the bar, Paige came in off the street wearing a filled backpack and carrying a smaller suitcase in her right hand. Steve didn't notice her until she reached his table.

"Hi," she said from beside his right shoulder, "what you doin'?"

He looked up, noticing the luggage.

"I might have known."

"What?" She took off the pack and sat down next to him.

"You're history."

"I've got to go."

"Your mom will kill me."

"Don't breathe a word of this to her."

"You know I won't, but she'd massacre me if she thought I was letting you out of my sight."

"I'm a big girl, I can take care of myself."

"I hope so."

"I'll see you in just a few days."

"I'm definitely staying on another week here. I love Cuernavaca and I need the Spanish."

"Okay, so in a week and a few days. I'll start snooping around the Serrano camp early for us."

"Just take it easy till Andres and I get there, all right?"

"All right." She put her hand on his arm.

He delicately extracted the arm and took a drink of beer. A group of laughing students came into *La Primavera* and sat noisily at a nearby table.

"Gonna buy me a going-away beer?"

"Sure, why the heck not?"

"You're a sweetheart."

Steve signaled down the bar to a chunky waiter who stood by an inner door. The waiter approached their table.

"*Dos mas cervezas, por favor.*"

"*Sí, señor.*" The waiter gave him a little bow before heading back toward the bar area.

"Very good." Paige congratulated Steve. "You're picking it up fast."

"Not fast enough. Not nearly fast enough."

"You understand why I have to do this, don't you?" Paige said after the waiter had brought their beers.

"I think I understand why you 'want' to do this, but I don't especially see why you 'have' to do it."

"I thought we were together on this thing." She sipped her beer and looked Steve straight in the eye.

"You know this has been your show since Day One," he parried. "I'm no more than your gofer, your cheerleader."

"This isn't about cheerleading."

"No? Then what is it about? You tell me."

"It's about us, about our careers, our futures."

"It's not about me at all. It's about you. And Jack Dodge. I wish I'd never heard of the damned guy."

"That's childish."

"Childish, my eye, what's childish is your attitude about him. You act like he was one of the Beatles or something. He's just a washed up writer. And that's all that he is."

"He's a lot more than that."

"How do you know? All you've seen is an old video and a bunch of ancient articles."

"It's in his books. If you'd bothered to read them, you'd know what I mean. He's really special."

"Aw, jeez, listen to yourself," Steve groaned. "You sound like a teeny bopper groupie. If I didn't know you better I'd think you're actually infatuated with this Dodge character even though you've never… well, I'll be damned.

You dig this jerk, don't you? You've never even laid eyes on the guy but you have a case on him. I'll be a son of a gun."

"Don't try to analyze me, Mr. Intro to Psych. You're not up to it."

"All right." Steve stopped laughing. "You don't have to trash me to justify your own behavior. You'll do what you want anyway." He downed the remaining beer and signaled the waiter for another.

"You don't have to do that because of me." Paige watched him immediately gulp down half of his next beer.

"I'm not doing it because of you. I'm doing it because of me."

She watched him hurriedly finish the beer. When he started to signal for the waiter again, she put her hand on his arm again. He looked down at it like it was a foreign object.

"Don't. I call a truce. I don't want to leave with us mad at each other."

"I'm not mad. I just want another beer."

"Finish mine." She set her beer in front of him. "I don't want it. Truce?"

"Truce."

"Wish me well?"

"You're pushing your luck."

"Wish me well?"

"What else can I do? Yes, I wish you well."

"You're a real friend." She leaned across the table and kissed him on the cheek. He looked away.

"I'm a real something," he muttered to the concrete floor of the bar. "A real something or other."

15

"Did you ever read *The Crying of Lot 49*, Mel?"

Dodge and West were with a handful of semi-permanent San Miguel gringos in the TV room of the *Texicana* Restaurant drinking beer and watching a cable baseball game from the states.

"No, can't say that I have. That's Pynchon, right? Another *yanqui* recluse."

"Yes, Thomas Pynchon, but not 'another' recluse, if you're referring to me. Pynchon really is a recluse. They say he only sees his agent or publisher in New York in the middle of the night, like three a.m. or something. Only one picture exists of him, maybe it's him, maybe it's not. Supposedly it's a real old one anyway."

"How about not seeing your agent or publisher in God knows how many years? Pynchon sounds like a wild extrovert compared to some people I know."

"Give it a rest, pal, you're not going to start a fight with me tonight. I'm too sober."

"You hear that, everyone?" West addressed the others in the room. "Jack Dodge, famous ex-writer, too sober to fight. Another first in San Miguel."

A couple of the regulars applauded.

"Entropy," Dodge said to West when he had his attention again.

"Entropy?"

"Pynchon deals with it. It has to do with the constant reduction of available energy in a closed thermodynamic system. Its social and psychological parallel would be something like ennui—emotional exhaustion, a sense of dissatisfaction, soul weariness."

"Sounds like practically every expatriate American in San Miguel, including ourselves."

"Exactly. The *gringo* culture here isn't vital or dynamic, it's entropic, shrinking in upon itself. Defeatism, depression, despair."

"Yeah, so what's your point?"

"The point is that we're trapped in this cycle, too," Dodge said.

"I wouldn't say *trapped*. I'd say we're the instruments of our own ineffectuality. We chose to come down here and we choose to stay."

"I won't argue that point, but once you're here it's hard to stay out of that entropic world. You end up like everybody else—nowhere, without hope, without direction, without energy."

"I repeat, what's your point, Jack? Is there some practical application of this theory?"

"Maybe, but you and I are like all these other deadheads down here, we've been inactive so long we no longer even consider doing anything."

"I thought that was the result of alcohol."

"You know what I mean."

"Yes," West allowed. "I guess that I do."

"Like with those jerks who took your notebook. We just accepted their taking it. Doing anything wasn't even considered. Wasn't an option."

"What, you gonna waltz into Mendoza's place and demand it back? Get serious, Jack."

"No, not that, but I am serious about you getting the stuff back. Go to Serrano, see if he can do anything for you."

"Hmm," West mused. "For the first time in Lord knows when, you might have come up with an idea."

"It was just something I was thinking about."

"All right. When we finish up here, you want to go up to Serrano's with me?"

"Not this afternoon. I promised Emma I'd go to the market with her."

"What's good for the philosopher is not good for the 'philosophee', or something like that?"

"Hell, you know the Serrano people better than I do anyway, you hardly need my help."

"That's true enough, you ready to cut out anyway?"

"Yeah." Dodge signaled to a waiter for their bill. "I need to get going. I'm on my best behavior with Emma."

"That'd be a first."

"Let's go. We got places to be and things to do."

"Also a first," West wisecracked as they walked out of the TV room. Dodge waved to their compatriots who remained in the room, tiredly watching the ball game. "Definitely a first."

"Up yours, Mel." Dodge led them single file out through the dark restaurant and into the bright afternoon sun.

They paused on the sidewalk for a moment, Dodge barely registering the sight of a young girl getting out of a taxi down the street to their right, then they turned left and headed up hill toward the *jardín.*

—

Paige arrived mid-afternoon at the bus station on the outskirts of San Miguel de Allende and immediately took a taxi up the hilly streets of the little *pueblo* to the San Pablo, a mid-range hotel two and a half short blocks below the *jardín.* The taxi driver helped pull her luggage from the trunk of the cab. Together they carried her things just inside the front door of the hotel, then returned to the sidewalk. Paige dug around in her bag for the fare and a tip for the taxi driver and as she did two middle-aged men exited a restaurant just up the cobblestone street from the San Pablo.

With barely a glance in her direction, the two men turned away and headed uphill toward the *jardín.* Below them on the street, Paige paid the driver, then turned back toward the hotel. She took in the retreating figures of the two men, something about the shorter of the two striking a memory she couldn't quite bring out, then stepped through the door and into the hotel. Inside, she found the young hotel clerk to be highly attentive.

"Yes, miss," the clerk answered in English after Paige inquired about a room in Spanish. "Will that be for one person?"

"Yes." The clerk brushed his hair back and gave Paige a big goofy smile. "Is there a restaurant also?"

"*Sí, señorita,* upstairs, to the back."

"They're open for supper tonight?"

"*Sí*, at five they open. For breakfast they open at seven and at twelve o'clock for lunch."

"Good. Thank you. And is there a phone I can use? Cell service down here is spotty at best."

"*Como no.*" The clerk dramatically pointed to a booth across from the counter. "You may use it to call the United States."

"I see."

"Over here, *señorita.*" The clerk swept his arm to the left where the room extended well beyond the counter to an elevated, carpeted area furnished with large chairs, a table or two, and a big TV. The walls were decorated with reproductions of paintings by local artists. "This is the TV room. It is open until eleven each night. Guests can watch TV here when they wish."

"Uh-huh, nice. Do I pay now?"

"When you wish, miss, you may pay also when you leave."

"Good." Paige let go of the charge card she was about to pull from her bag. "I'll pay later, then."

"*Muy bien.*" the clerk reached behind to his left and pulled a key from a slot and handed it to Paige. He managed to briefly touch her hand as he did.

"One last question." She pulled her hand away.

"I am at your service." The clerk wiggled his eyebrows.

"Can you tell me where the Serrano campaign headquarters are?"

"Of course."

He pulled out a little map of San Miguel and put it on the counter. With an index finger, he traced the route.

"We are here. You go up the street to the *jardín*, the square, then cross it and up two more blocks. Take a right and the headquarters is right there. You can't miss it."

"May I have this map?"

"Naturally, please take it."

"Thank you." Paige folded the map and put it in her bag.

—

After she rested and freshened up, Paige went in search of the Serrano campaign headquarters. She made her way through San Miguel's steep, narrow streets, passing through the *jardín* and by the *Parroquia*, then uphill through a gawking mix of locals and tourists.

Turning right onto the first street beyond the *jardín*, a particularly narrow one, she had to move to one side to allow a *campesino* and his burro pass. She made a journalist's mental note that while the *campesino* and his wood-laden burro were a part of modern San Miguel, they remained a living reminder of Mexico's less hectic, less urban past.

She continued up the street to a big doorway on the left that opened into a courtyard within which the Serrano headquarters was located in a busy three room office. Decorations in the windows and on outer walls and a huge Serrano for President sign above the front door testified to the accuracy of the San Pablo clerk's map. Putting on her best newspaperwoman attitude, Paige stepped boldly inside.

Within the chaotic headquarters, her attention was immediately drawn to a table at one side of the room where a tall, thin *gringo* was complaining to an important looking Mexican man about somebody called Mendoza whose thugs had taken his writing notebook. Although the room was full of busy people, she managed to stay unobtrusively in the background. She listened intently to the conversation between the two men.

"I'd go get the damn thing back myself," the tall man said, "but those idiots'd probably kick my butt all over the place this time."

"It was just a notebook?"

"Yeah, but I had notes in there for practically the whole last six months. A lot of it's personal. Some of it political."

"Now with the elections getting so close, Mendoza will be dangerous. He's afraid his stooges will lose. You shouldn't go over there."

"No kidding. But I want it back."

The Mexican man looked up and noticed Paige watching them. The tall man turned around to see what he was looking at.

"Leave it to me, Mel." The Mexican man distractedly ended their conversation. "I'll try to get your things back."

"That's what I was hoping, Enrique…" Mel began, as Enrique stepped over to greet Paige.

"*Buenas tardes, señorita.*" Enrique greeted the new arrival. "How may I help you?"

"Hi, I'm Paige Warren." She showed the press credentials Jean Holland had provided. Enrique waved them off as if they were unnecessary among reputable professionals. "I'm an intern for the *Mexico City Times* and they sent me to San Miguel to get background on the coalition and, I hope, an interview with Mr. Serrano."

"Paige Warren, oh, yes, Jean, uh…."

"Holland. Jean Holland."

"*Sí,* Jean Holland called us that you would be coming. But wasn't there someone else supposed to be with you?"

"Yes, my photographer. But he's still in Cuernavaca studying Spanish. I left early to come on to San Miguel."

"*¿Oh, entonces,*" Enrique went into Spanish, "*habla usted Español?*"

"*Poquito.*" Paige used the standard *gringo* answer translating to Mexican ears as "no." Enrique shifted back to English.

"Very good."

"And you are?"

"Oh, I'm sorry. I am Enrique Serrano. Rolando's brother."

"Wonderful. Will you be able to help me?"

"Certainly. We have already prepared material for you and we have books and, how do you say, pamphlets here, too."

"Great. That's terrific. Is your brother—er—Mr. Serrano, here today?"

"No, he is out of town just now."

"Will I be able to get an interview with him?"

"I'm sure that that can be arranged, *señorita*. He will be back in a few days. We will set something up then."

"Thank you, Mr. Serrano."

"Enrique, please. Call me Enrique."

"Thank you, Enrique. You're very kind and helpful."

"We want to help. This is a great time for my brother, for San Miguel, for Mexico. We want everyone to see that Mexico is changing, that we are democratic and becoming a great nation." He signaled to a young boy to bring over a stack of books and papers from a table across the room.

"I can see that you do."

The boy hurried over with the pile of information. He handed it to Enrique with a shy smile for Paige.

"*Gracias, muchacho*. Here, Miss Warren."

Paige collected the stack, nearly dropping some of it. Mel reached out to catch some of the material and then helped her get the stack in order.

"Thank you, sir."

"Think nothing of it."

They set the papers on the table near where Mel had been giving his complaint to Enrique. Paige sat down and began perfunctorily rummaging through the information. The two men remained standing, watching her.

"I'm Melville West, by the way."

"Oh, I'm sorry, Mel," Enrique apologized, "how rude of me. Miss Warren, this is Mel West. He's one of San Miguel's permanent North Americans."

"Nice to meet you, Mr. West." She offered her hand, which he shook firmly. "You must be a writer with a name like that."

"I write, but not books. I just write."

"I understand San Miguel has a lot of expatriate artists and writers. "Is that true?"

"Oh, yes, indeed, miss," Enrique confirmed.

"And do they have a particular place they like to hang out?"

"Depends on the particular one you might be looking for," West said.

"How specific do I have to get?"

"Well, do you want a short one, a fat one, a rich one, a burnt out one?"

"The last kind."

"There's several to choose from."

"How about one who might have been well known once but then kind of dropped off the edge of the earth."

"If I knew a guy that fit that description." West raised an eyebrow and gave Enrique a quick look. "I'd say he'd hang out in a dingy bar, like maybe one called *El Infiernito*."

"*El Infiernito*? Doesn't that mean little hell?"

"That's what it would be."

"There's really a place like that here, and called that?"

"*Señorita*," Enrique said, "a lady should not go to a place like *El Infiernito*."

"Oh, no? And exactly why not?"

"Definitely not," West agreed. "Probably not a good place for a lady."

"Well." Paige gave West a look that caused him to look away and shuffle around uncomfortably. "Thank you both for the information and the warning. I'll take them under advisement."

"We're here to serve," Enrique said.

"I'm sure you are." Paige said.

She then turned her attention to the pile of Serrano campaign material. Enrique winked at West. West took out a handkerchief and wiped his brow. Paige grinned happily at nothing in particular.

"Yes," she mouthed silently, "yes!"

16

"This country," Andres explained to Steve, as they neared the beautiful southern city of Oaxaca, "is that of the Zapotec and Mixtec. Benito Juarez was Zapotec."

"The famous president?"

"*Sí.* A great favorite of the people." Andres pointed to the west. "Up there, on top of that mountain are the ruins of Monte Alban. You must visit them."

"I want to."

As they drove into Oaxaca proper, Andres gave Steve a quick tour, ending up at the ubiquitous *zocalo*, or city center, which was another *jardín* similar to, but somewhat larger than, the one in San Miguel.

"Notice a thing different here in the Oaxaca *zocalo*?"

"No. What?"

"The church. See it is not facing the *zocalo* like most but is off to the side there. Different."

"I see now," Steve said, as Andres found a place to park.

"We'll check into the hotel now. Tomorrow is the big Serrano rally and we will be busy then. Later we can get something to eat and I will show you around. The big *mercado* is only a couple of blocks away."

"Yes," Steve agreed, "I will. Sounds great."

—

Early the next afternoon, they attended the Serrano Rally held in the plaza fronting the big cathedral at the side of the *zocalo*. The area had been colorfully decorated for the whirlwind campaign stop, and the candidate thrilled the responsive crowd with a rousing speech calling for sweeping land reform throughout Mexico.

As the mostly happy crowd dispersed after the speech, Steve and Andres moved among them on the edge of the plaza passing by the grocery and record stores, the magazine vendors, and the overflowing outdoor cafes. Laden with camera gear, Steve was flushed and talkative, as they neared the hotel where Serrano's people had temporarily set up shop.

"Andres, man, thanks for bringing me down here, this is great. Oaxaca's a terrific town and this rally was excellent."

"I know it was a long way to come, but—"

"Oh, no, I got all kinds of photos and info for Paige. This was outstanding. Rolando was great. I just know he's going to win."

"Maybe some of the pictures will be used for tomorrow's edition of the *Times*."

"No kidding? That would be amazing."

"Sure, why not."

"Outstanding," Steve said, as they reached the far side of the plaza away from the cathedral.

They turned right at the corner and walked a few yards down the street to the hotel. Inside, there were still a few Serrano people around and while Andres stopped at the desk for messages, Steve went into a room off the lobby being used by the Serrano camp as their temporary headquarters. As he came into the room, his photography gear clanking together, two men quickly exited through a back door. Surprised, he called after them thinking they were Serrano's workers.

"Hey, wait." He saw a large piece of paper, apparently hastily tacked to the wall, fall to the floor. "You dropped something."

When the men did not return, he went over and picked up the paper. Behind him, Andres came into the room. Steve opened the paper to see a photo of Serrano with a thick black line across it and beneath the photo the words: Muerte al Comunista. He was puzzling over the words when Andres reached his side.

"Andres, what does this mean exactly?"

Andres looked the paper over, eyes widening as he read.

"Where did this come from?"

Before Steve could answer, a group of rowdy, happy Serrano people poured into the room. At their head was portly, red-faced campaign manager, Diego Salazar. Andres waved to Salazar, who came right over.

"What is it, Andres?"

"You should see this, Diego." Andres pointed to the piece of paper.

"I came in just as two men were leaving out the back." Steve handed the paper to Salazar.

"Uh-huh." After a moment Salazar folded the paper and pocketed it. "It is a bad joke, nothing more. A stupidity."

"Shouldn't we tell Mr. Serrano?"

"No, no, he has too much to think about already."

"But it could be something dangerous."

"These things happen all the time." Salazar described the reality of Mexican political life. "They are hoaxes. Some foolish game."

"It doesn't seem foolish to me."

"You are new here?" Salazar directed his full attention to Steve.

Andres answered for Steve. "He is a student working for us at the paper."

"Of course, you are unfamiliar with our ways. I assure you there's no reason to worry."

"I just wanted to be sure someone knew about it."

"I know about it," Salazar said authoritatively, "you did well. It will be noted. Thank you."

"Well, okay."

"I'll take care of it."

"Come on, Steve," Andres said, "let's go have a beer."

"Yeah, sure, sounds great."

"Good day, gentlemen," Salazar said.

Andres led Steve out of the room. Stone-faced, Salazar watched them go.

17

Early one pleasant evening during the second week of her stay in San Miguel, Paige decided to have supper at an airy little greasy spoon café whose main point of recommendation was that it was directly across the street from the front door of *El Infiernito* bar.

The night life of San Miguel was just beginning, and an array of cleaned up locals, students, and tourists passed by while Paige, hardly noticing them as she slowly consumed a plate of mediocre cheese enchiladas swimming in grease, seldom took her eye off *El Infiernito.*

Mercifully, halfway through the second *enchilada* her patience paid off, for emerging from the smoky dimness of *El Infiernito* came Mel West with a man she recognized with a thrill as a matured Jack Dodge.

Laughing, the two men turned left and headed uptown. Paige tossed down her fork and enough pesos to cover the meal and a tip and, after giving the men a little bit of a head start, followed them in the direction of the *jardín.*

She carefully tailed the men as they trudged along. They were obviously a little inebriated and apparently oblivious to anything around them. At the lower corner of the plaza they stopped, exchanged a few words that she could not hear and then went their separate ways. West to the left, across the plaza and up the hilly streets away from downtown, Dodge straight ahead down the sidewalk across the street from the *Parróquia*. Paige followed Dodge. When he was about even with the front side of the church, he suddenly ducked into a bar and disappeared.

She hurried after him.

Looking at the sign above the bar entrance, she recognized it as a trendy hangout for expatriate artists called *La Selva Oscura*. She stepped into an inner hallway that opened up into the large, active bar and dining area beyond. Without warning, Dodge popped out, cat-like, from a darkened doorway to her right.

"Ooh." She stepped back from him. "You scared me."

"Sorry about that." He eyed her suspiciously.

"Do you always do that to people?" She caught her breath from the fright. Dodge took a moment to check her over carefully, clearly enjoying what he saw.

"Are you following me?"

"Well, sort of."

"Sort of? Why? Who are you?"

"You don't know me."

"That's right. I don't know you."

"Well, actually, yes, you do, sort of."

"Sort of? You were sort of following me? I sort of know you?"

"It's a long story."

"I can relate to long stories," Dodge said. "Suppose we have a beer and you tell me your long story?"

"All right."

Paige followed as he led them into the interior of the bar.

La Selva Oscura was like a church for drinkers. At the back center was a stage for bands to perform beneath twenty foot high ceilings, which were spotted here and there with ineffectual Havana fans. Surrounding the stage to the left and right were rows of heavy, pew-like wood tables with matching heavy, leather-backed chairs. At left center was a large, open doorway leading to a smaller group of tables that provided at least some semblance of privacy in the quite social bar.

Dodge led them to the private area but not before he was greeted by all of the bartenders, waitresses, and half or more of the clientele. Paige marveled at this when they had settled comfortably at a table and ordered a round of beers.

"You must know everyone in San Miguel. That's surprising to me."

"Surprising? In case you haven't noticed, young lady, San Miguel is a pretty small town."

"Not the kind of place you'd expect somebody to try to hide in, is it?"

"People here don't care who you are."

"Is that what you want, for people not to care who you are?"

"You look familiar to me." Dodge said.

"You probably say that to every young girl you meet."

"I never say anything to girls that I don't mean, whether I've met them or not."

"Never?"

"Never."

"I'll remember that."

"Try remembering who you are and why you were looking for me," Dodge said. "I have other things yet to do tonight."

"My name is Paige."

"Just Paige?"

"For now."

"Okay, Just-Paige-For-Now, what's up? I'm not young anymore like you, I don't have unlimited time to waste on word games."

Before Paige could answer, a waiter arrived with the beer. When he had gone and they each had a drink, the conversation resumed.

"I know who you are," she said.

"I know who I am, too. What of it?"

"I came here to find you."

"I've been here for a long time."

"Time enough to forget whatever it was that drove you down here in the first place?"

"Listen Paige, whoever you are," Dodge said, "you're a bright girl and witty—but what's the angle, what are you up to? Let's cut the bull. I'm really not in the mood to do this all night."

"I'm not BS'ing you."

"Then talk straight to me."

"I did come here to find you."

"Maybe you think I'm somebody else?"

"No, Mr. Dodge, I—"

"Jack, the name is Jack. Mr. Dodge is my dad, or was."

"I recognized you from photos. You haven't changed that much."

"That's a matter of opinion." He signaled the waiter for another beer. Paige waved off the offer.

"What do you want," Dodge continued, "to blow my cover? People know who I am here. They don't care. Or did you come down to drag me back to the craphole world I left years ago. Is that it? Are you my savior?"

"I'm a journalist, a student journalist. We came down here to cover the elections. You're the secondary reason."

"Now I'm secondary, huh? How flattering. And who's *we*?"

"Steve Thompson, my photographer. He'll be coming up soon from Cuernavaca."

"Oh, I get it. You're here to get the exclusive story. *Where Are They Now—Expatriate Writer Down and Out in Mexico.* Who do you work for, *The Enquirer?*"

"I'm working as an intern for the *Mexico City Times*, but I really just wanted to find you, to see you, to talk to you. I want to know why."

"Why what?"

"Why what? My God, Mr., er, Jack..." She paused a moment. Dodge pounded down his second beer and looked at his watch. "Didn't anyone else ever come looking for you?"

"At first they did, but I scared them off. Like I'm doing you. Eventually they stopped coming. Is that enough for you, for tonight?"

"But you were such a wonderful writer. How could you just—just *desert* everyone like that?"

"So I'm a big failure," he said gruffly. "It's as simple as that. What else do you want from me?" He looked around the bar and drummed his fingers nervously on the table. "In some quarters being a failed writer will get you a lot of mileage."

"I don't buy into that failure crap. It might work on some people, it won't for me."

"I don't want to talk about this anymore." Dodge started to get up. "I should go. This is stupid."

"Please." Paige motioned for him to stay. "We can talk about something else if you'd like. I didn't mean to upset you."

"It's okay." He looked away from her. "I've got to go. I promised some friends I'd drop by."

"But we barely got started."

"Yeah, well...." He scooted his chair back.

"Please don't go. I don't mean to hurt you. I just want to get to know you."

"I can't do this anymore." He rose from his chair. "I don't remember how it goes from here."

"Can I please see you again?" She reached for his arm.

"It's a small town." He pulled back. "But I...."

"I won't ask you anything else," she promised, "honest."

Dodge continued to edge away. Paige had never seen a grown man look so frightened over a conversation.

"No, it's okay, really. I've gotta run. Good night, I'm sorry."

"Jack, wait...."

"I'm sorry." Dodge turned and abruptly walked away. Stunned, Paige watched him go.

"Damn it."

Several nearby patrons turned to look at her. In the inner room, a band began to play loud *norteño* music. Paige sipped on her beer and stared straight ahead at the wall.

18

Next morning after the unsettling meeting with Dodge, Paige felt as tired as she ever had before. She breakfasted at the San Pablo's second floor restaurant and sat at a table near the back. She tentatively dug her fork once or twice into a plate of anemic bacon strips and bright yellow scrambled eggs.

After a little more probing, she settled instead for a drink of strong, black coffee. Just then, Steve Thompson entered the restaurant's main doors. She watched him look around the room. He finally spotted her in his peripheral vision and with a big smile hurried over.

"Hey," he called out.

"Did you just get in?" She stood and hugged him.

"Yeah and, boy, is it good to see you again."

"Me, too, are you checked in and everything already?"

"Yeah, neat old hotel, huh?"

"I guess so." A waiter came up for Steve's order.

"Just a glass of orange juice, please."

He turned his attention back to Paige. "You feeling bad?"

"I've been putting in some late hours this week." She held her cup of coffee in both hands and sipped it slowly.

"Me, too. Andres and I covered Serrano's campaign stop in Oaxaca."

"I didn't know you did that. That's great. How did it go down there?"

"Terrific. Got some great shots. The *Times* has already used a couple of them. I have plenty more for you, though. And some background material."

"Good." Paige set her coffee down. "We can use it for the next couple of articles I'm working on."

"Good deal."

"Things are moving now, the election's nearly here."

"I'd say. We got a death threat or something in Oaxaca."

"What? A death threat? To you personally?"

"No, I think it was meant for Serrano. His campaign manager Salazar just blew it off, but I think it was serious."

"I haven't met this Salazar." Paige wrinkled her brow.

"I didn't much like him. Too smooth for me."

"Yeah, well, whatever, you just be careful. My research up here shows me that the Mexican elections can sometimes get a little hairy. Especially when there's a particularly strong outside party, like Serrano's."

"That goes for you, too."

"It's been quiet here in San Miguel. Mostly, anyway."

"So, did you find the great mystery man writer?"

"As a matter of fact," Paige said. "I did."

"What? He's really still here after all this time?"

"We even had a drink at a bar."

"You're kidding me. What was he like, weird?"

"He's different. I wouldn't say he's weird."

The waiter arrived with Steve's juice.

"Thank you."

"*Por nada*. Will there be anything else, sir?"

"Not for me." The waiter looked at Paige.

"No, thank you."

"So," Steve said, when the waiter had gone, "what about Dodge? What did you talk about?"

"We had kind of an odd, silly sort of conversation. Then he seemed to get real freaked out about the whole thing and just took off."

"Took off?"

"Uh-huh. He was being kind of glib, even flirty, then poof, he changed and was out the door on me."

"You don't call that weird?"

"It was like he was carrying a lot of pain around inside. He had the saddest eyes I've ever seen."

"Oh, brother."

"Don't say it, Steve."

"I'm only concerned about you. This is sort of obsessive behavior you're showing with this Dodge guy."

"You sound like a mother hen. My mother hen to be exact."

"Your mother wouldn't want you to get into something over your head, or get hurt," Steve protested. "And neither would I."

"I'm grown, Mommy. I mean Stevie. I can take care of myself."

"Yes, but—"

"No buts, cut it out right now or I'm gonna make a fuss and embarrass the devil out of you."

"You wouldn't."

Steve looked around the restaurant at the watchful waiter and a handful of other breakfasters. Paige shifted in her seat in preparation for some sort of public display.

"Try this on," she warned.

"All right, all right," he acquiesced. "I'm sorry. You win again, as usual."

"That's my Steve. Now relax and drink your juice. Later I'll take you up to Serrano headquarters."

"Jack Dodge may not be so easily manipulated, you know."

"I guess we'll have to see about that one, won't we?"

"I guess you will. I just guess you will."

19

On her way back to the hotel after visiting Serrano headquarters, Paige spotted Mel West sitting on a bench in the plaza reading a copy of the *Mexico City Times*.

"Hello, Mr. West."

"Uh-huh."

In the late afternoon sun his features formed a noncommittal mask.

"Have you seen Jack Dodge by any chance? I'm looking for him."

"Ain't seen him."

"You're his best friend, aren't you? Do you know where he is?"

"I don't think Dodge has a best friend." West laid the paper down. "But I suppose I'm the closest thing to one. You'll find him where I said you could the first time you ever asked."

"At that bar, the *Infiernito*? Right now, this time of day?" West shrugged. "Well, thank you, Mr. West."

"Better save your thanks till after you've seen him, maybe then you won't feel the same." He picked up his paper and continued reading.

"Thank you anyway," Paige said to the backside of the newspaper, "good-bye."

"Uh-huh."

—

Steve rose early to roam San Miguel's rocky streets in search of interesting people and places to photograph, but ended up mostly soaking up the rich atmosphere of the tiny *pueblo*. About ten-thirty, as he walked a few short blocks from the central plaza he passed several small kiosks, remnants of an earlier outdoor *mercado*.

He had paused at one of the kiosks for a moment when suddenly a little boy appeared and tugged on his arm. The child pushed a folded piece of paper into his hand, pointed at the large double-doored entrance of a nearby church and then rushed away, quickly vanishing down a side street.

Taken aback, Steve stayed by the kiosk for a few moments considering what to do. Finally, he walked across the church courtyard, found a space of his own among the "miracle" vendors and the devout and checked out the paper the little boy had thrust on him. He was stunned to see the same message he had found in Oaxaca—*Muerte al Comunista*. He carefully folded the paper, looked around, and then headed into the church.

Inside the cool, dark building, he slowly surveyed the interior of the church with its many candles and icons. There were several penitents kneeling and praying as well. There was a movement to his right behind a confessional.

"Hello?"

When no answer was forthcoming, he walked toward the confessional. Just as he reached it, the door on the priest's side clicked shut. He took the cue but cautiously entered the other side, shutting the door softly. There was a pause as he waited breathlessly for whatever was going to happen next. All he could see through the priest's side was an unidentifiable figure in shadows. Finally the figure spoke—with a heavy accent.

"You want to find those who threatened Serrano?"

"Yes," Steve whispered.

"You know the House of the Inquisitor?"

"I can find it."

"Come at sunset if you want to know. Alone."

Before he could say anything else, there was movement on the other side of the confessional, and the door clicked open again.

"Wait! Come on, what is this about?"

"Be there," the voice said menacingly, and then with a rustle the figure belonging to it vanished out the back of the confessional.

"This is getting strange." Steve rubbed the back of his neck with his right hand.

Back outside, he squinted into the sunlight and was surprised by a man who appeared from around the side of the church and nearly bumped into him. Steve stopped abruptly to avoid the collision.

The man walked away quickly without speaking or looking up. Steve noted the man's thick-bodied amble, his barrel chest and pot belly, but couldn't see his face under the pork pie hat he had pulled down low on his forehead.

"I gotta tell Paige about this," he said out loud. A shiver of fear and excitement ran down his spine. "She'll never believe it."

—

Paige stood in front of El Infiernito for several moments trying to decide whether to enter or not. Finally, after a couple of tentative moves toward and away from the bar, she squared her shoulders and entered with resolve.

Inside, it was smoky and dark, lit up occasionally by a flashing red neon sign above the bar. Paige paused just inside the door to let her eyes adapt to the light, or lack of it. In a moment, she was able to see the interior of the shabby little bar.

At center left was the bar itself, behind which a woman was working. To the immediate left and right were several tables at which a few patrons sat. Despite all the forewarnings from Mel West and Enrique Serrano, her entrance seemed to have roused little interest.

She scanned the rest of the room and saw Jack Dodge sitting alone at a bottle-filled table to the back right of the bar. She headed straight toward him. He looked up just as she reached the table.

"Whad'ya say, girlie?" he said loudly. "Come lookin' for the old gringo again, eh? Pull up a chair, missy, and have a drink. We don't often get young girls here in little hell, do we, Emma? Hey, Emma, bring us a couple of beers. That's okay, isn't it, uh, Paige?"

"Yes, that's fine." She sat down across from him.

Emma came over from behind the bar with the beers and set them down on the table.

"Put 'em on my tab," Dodge told her.

"Your tab is as big as your ego, Jack Dodge, and as big as it can get." Emma gave Paige a long once-over. Paige quickly came up with *pesos* for the beers and handed them over. Emma winked at her. "Thanks, honey, it's nice to see real money around the place for a change." Dodge snorted.

"Thank you," Paige said.

"What for?" Emma said. "After I rescue you from this thing, then you might have a reason to thank me."

"Thank you, barmaid." Jack dismissed Emma. "Thank you very much. That will be all."

Emma flipped him off and went back behind the bar where she pretended not to watch or listen to the proceedings at the table.

"That wasn't nice," Paige told Dodge.

"I'm not a nice person."

"You don't have to pretend you're not for me."

"Oh, I never pretend."

"You never lie. You never pretend. You're—"

"What do you want from me? What are you doing here? Jesus."

"Just talk. You ran out so fast the other night we never had the chance to get to know one another."

"Why would you want to know me?"

"There are a lot of questions I'd like to ask."

"Didn't you promise not to ask me any more questions the other night?"

"That was then, this is now."

"Okay, go ahead and ask."

"The obvious question is why did you do it?"

"Do it? Do what?" He stared into Paige's eyes.

She pushed back her thick brown hair with a tan, slender hand, the movement not wasted on Dodge. Her presence seemed to be sobering him up, but also agitating him, as it had before.

"Why did you turn down the Pulitzer Prize? It's such a prestigious award."

"Did I do that? I don't remember anymore. I thought they just didn't give an award that year."

"It would have meant so much to your career." Paige consciously repeated the questions of the interviewer she'd seen on tape. "Money. Celebrity. Status. What were you thinking at the time? Where were you coming from?"

"I was coming from left field. That's obvious enough now, isn't it?"

"I guess, but—"

"But they would have wanted me to get up in front of a bunch of dodo heads in suits and ties and tell them what a great award they give out, what a wonderful, free nation we live in, how the human spirit will endure."

"And you couldn't do that?"

"Hell, no. And why should I? It's a bunch of crap. Lies."

"I guess I don't have to ask you if you still feel the same."

"That's right, you don't."

"Don't you think things can change? Don't you think you could? I thought you were a man of ideals and action."

"Who told you such drivel?"

"You did."

Dodge didn't seem so drunk anymore and to Paige he acted like someone who'd been waiting a long time to get something off his chest. That was what she had hoped for.

"Me? What are you talking about?"

"It's in your books and interviews."

"Ancient history."

"So now you're not active, you don't write, and you're apolitical. That's a long way from where you used to be, isn't it?"

"Is this conversation going somewhere or are you just in here to soak up the atmosphere?"

"I don't buy this bitter recluse act, Jack. I think you're the same man who wrote those wonderful books and stood up for his principles. I don't believe that you've given up on everything."

Dodge gulped down the rest of his beer and started on Paige's, which she had barely touched. She reached out and held his hand against the bottle, stopping him from drinking. For a moment they were quiet, staring into each other's eyes. Then Dodge pulled the beer away and took a drink. When he spoke again, he was distant, cold.

"Maybe I was a believer, once."

"You're still a believer. I know you are."

"How would you know? You don't know anything about me. Don't tell me about living. I've seen plenty. You're just a kid."

"So you're the big writer disappointed by life. You have some personal defeats, then reject your greatest victory and run off to hide. You're not a principled expatriate or a great writer, you're just a big coward. You're pathetic."

Emma, responding to the rising voices, came out from behind the bar and walked toward their table.

"Bravo, little miss journalist," Dodge exulted with a staged laugh. He leaned back in his chair and clapped his hands. "I see you have that youthful quality of knowing everything there is to know, don't you? Well, let me tell you something, little girl—"

"Stop calling me that."

"Excuse me, missy."

"You want to stay down here wallowing in self-pity, drinking yourself to death, go for it. You're just crass and stupid. You don't want to be happy."

Emma came up to the table and stood by Paige's right shoulder, all the while giving Dodge the evil eye.

"Maybe you should go." He looked from Paige to Emma, "both of you."

"Come on, honey." Emma put her hand gently on Paige's shoulder. "Don't let this jerk get to you. He just wants everybody to hurt like he does."

"Everybody's a philosopher," Dodge snorted.

"I thought you would be like your books," Paige said, eyes welling up.

Dodge looked away from her. Paige let Emma help her up.

"He's forgotten who that man was, baby. Let him stew in his own juices."

Dodge tried to sneer rakishly at the women, but his tough guy act looked more like a hurt little boy than a world-weary, mature adult. Paige and Emma walked away from him. He rubbed the back of his neck and looked down sheepishly at the floor.

"Have a drink on me, hon," Emma said when she and Paige were back by the bar. "Forget that old fart."

"Thank you, no." Paige tried to laugh through her emotions. "I'm just going to go back to my hotel."

"Sure?" Emma offered her a napkin.

"Sure." Paige dried her eyes.

"Don't pay any attention to him. He doesn't know how to show his feelings, that's all. He's out of practice."

"Doesn't seem it to me."

"I think you woke something up in him that's been asleep a long time. Honey, I haven't seen Jack Dodge this passionate about anything in a long time. I think he's that afraid of you. Scared to death."

"Afraid?"

"Of what you're waking up inside him. Things he hasn't felt in years."

Paige stared at Emma in amazement, then turned to look at Dodge. He wouldn't look over.

"Thanks, Emma." Paige appreciatively patted her hand. "Thanks a lot."

With a smile, Paige turned and strode out of *El Infiernito.* Emma watched the door where she had gone, then turned her attention back to Dodge. He steadfastly refused to look at her. In a while, she gave up glaring and busied herself cleaning the counter. Dodge stayed at his table, not drinking, staring straight ahead into the murky air of the bar at nothing.

—

After his strange experience at the church, Steve wanted to immediately tell Paige, but he couldn't locate her anywhere. Because of the spotty coverage in the area, he'd given up trying her cell phone and knowing her nature he figured she might not even have it turned on.

He assumed she would be out working, so he didn't bother to go by the San Pablo and check there, opting instead to drop by Serrano headquarters first. Not finding her there, he only stayed long enough to find a note from Andres tacked to a board near the desk that he, Paige, and several other Serrano workers shared.

The note was not particularly clear, but he made out that he was to meet Andres and Enrique Serrano at *El Puente* as soon as possible. They were waiting for him and jumped up when he came in.

"Oh, it's good you're here," Andres greeted him, "we have to hurry. We have to be there as soon as possible."

"Whoa, hey, Andres, have to be where as soon as possible?"

"Guanajuato, this is important."

"I have something imp—" Steve began but was interrupted by Enrique.

"Steve, this is, as Andres says, an important opportunity for us. A, how do you call it, photo opportunity. There has been a spontaneous *campesino* rally for Rolando called for this afternoon and we must get there right away. It's a chance we can't let go by. I hope you understand our need to hurry."

"Sure," Steve said, "sounds exciting to me. Are we taking off right now?"

"*Inmediatamente*," Andres said, "immediately."

Steve did a quick check of his gear and satisfied he had all the lenses and such that he would need, joined Enrique and Andres by the front door of *El Puente.*

"I'm all ready," he told them as they stepped outside where two cars had pulled up by the curb. "Who do I ride with?"

"Why don't you ride with me?" Diego Salazar said from the rider's side of the back vehicle.

Steve almost jumped at the sight and sound of Salazar. San Miguel really was too small, he told himself, this guy was creepy.

"Maybe I should go with Andres and Enrique," he mildly protested.

"No, no." Salazar pushed the rear door open. "I insist. Join us."

Steve looked helplessly at Andres and Enrique. Andres frowned but Enrique waved him on.

"Go on with Diego. We'll see you in Guanajuato."

"Great." Steve reluctantly climbed into the backseat of Salazar's car. "Just terrific."

"Have you ever been to Guanajuato?" Salazar asked when the vehicles had cleared San Miguel and were on Highway 110 heading out of town.

"No," Steve answered tersely, trying to get a good view of the man driving—the man had a hat pulled down low over his forehead and never took his eyes off the road. "I've never had the chance to go before."

"Then you'll love it. It is a beautiful city."

"Uh, yes. I'm sure it is."

—

To Steve's chagrin, Salazar dogged him the entire time in Guanajuato, putting on a supercilious show of helpfulness and good will that made him cringe. The *campesino* rally itself went off without a hitch, and though it would have been much better if Rolando had been there, Steve got some excellent shots of Enrique and Salazar with the completely unpretentious leader of the local movement.

Back in San Miguel later in the day, he only wanted one thing and that was to get out of that vehicle with the campaign manager and try and see Paige. As soon as they got near the plaza, he practically leaped out of the car and with the briefest of goodbyes and a quick wave to Enrique and Andres in the trailing car, Steve hurried back downhill to the San Pablo.

"Is *Señorita* Warren in?" His voice was breathless as he spoke to the young clerk behind the check-in counter.

"Let me see, sir." The clerk made a slow production of looking for her room key slot. Right away Steve could see her key was in the slot and that the clerk could see as well, but he patiently waited for the young man to confirm that she was out. "The *señorita* is not in."

"Do you know where she might be?"

"No, *señor,* she did not say."

"Can I leave a message?"

"*Como no.*"

The clerk produced a pad of paper and a pencil. Steve quickly scribbled his note and handed it to the clerk.

"Please give this to her."

"Of course."

With a curt nod, Steve wheeled and hurried out of the San Pablo. The clerk put the note on the counter and watched him go.

Outside, Steve looked up and down the street, not knowing exactly what to do or where to go. After a moment of indecision he turned left, back up the hill toward the plaza.

—

At sunset, Mel West strolled back from *El Puente,* taking the long way to his cluttered apartment in order to enjoy the onset of the cool evening. As he walked along a tiny cobblestone street, he passed a whitewashed building with a sign on one wall that read—House of the Inquisitor. Glancing over at the building, he was surprised to see a face appear in the window for just the briefest flash. It was a face he was sure he knew. A face with a long scar above the right eyebrow. He stopped for a moment and watched the window, but the face did not reappear.

About halfway down the street, still puzzling over the apparition-like visage, he made way for a young North American who was obviously searching for something. He paused and watched the young man stop in front of the House of the Inquisitor. The young man tried the door on the centuries-old house a couple of times and then suddenly disappeared within. West stared at the empty doorway for a few moments more then, scratching his head, continued on his walk.

—

The young clerk was still behind the counter at the San Pablo when Paige came in a little after dark.

"Excuse me."

"*Si, señorita.*"

"May I have my key, please."

"*Por supuesto.*"

The clerk reached back to the key slots behind him and handed her the key. She took it and headed toward the door. The clerk suddenly remembered Steve's note which he had failed to put in the key slot. It was still on the counter where he had left it. Quickly retrieving the note, he hurried to catch up to Paige.

"Oh, miss," he called, "miss, excuse me."

"Yes?" She stopped and turned back.

"This message is for you."

"For me?"

"Yes, the young man. Your friend?"

"Steve?" She took the note.

"Yes, I think so. He was here before looking for you."

The clerk gave a slight bow and went back behind the counter. Paige stepped into the outer hallway and read the note.

"On to something big, maybe. Will tell you about it later, Steve."

She scanned the message again.

"What are you up to now, Steve?" She neatly folded the message, put it in her bag and headed upstairs to her room.

20

The Serrano for President Headquarters was a beehive of activity. Busy workers crowded around tables and others scurried back and forth, arms laden with paperwork. In the central room in back of the building, Rolando and Enrique Serrano talked animatedly with the campaign manager, Diego Salazar. To the right in back, in another room, Paige pored over a pile of papers scattered on a table in front of her.

In the midst of the bustling activity, the front door opened and Jack Dodge entered, looking sober and subdued. From the back center room, Rolando saw Dodge and he and his brother came out to greet the expatriate writer. Salazar remained in the room, thumbing through an itinerary listing.

"Jack," Rolando cried, "old friend. How are you?"

"Hello, Rolando, Enrique."

"Jack." Enrique pumped his hand. "*Cómo estás?*"

"Asi, asi."

"It's been a while, Jack," Rolando noted, "have you at last come over to our side? To write about us for the American press?"

"I've always been on your side, Rolando, ever since I've been down here."

"Of course you have."

Salazar made his way from the back room and came up beside Enrique. Dodge saw that Salazar was carrying what looked like the notebook Mendoza's thugs had taken from Mel West. He scanned the cover of the notebook to be sure.

"Where did this come from?" he said to Salazar.

"I believe this belongs to your friend," Salazar said. "The tall, skinny one."

"*Madre,*" Enrique exclaimed. "I forgot all about that. I told Mel I would get it back for him."

"Where did you get this?" Dodge took the notebook. He eyed Salazar suspiciously.

"I have a brother-in-law with the police."

"Hmm." Dodge checked the notebook. It didn't look any worse for wear.

"Jack, would you like an interview?" Rolando put his hand on Dodge's shoulder. "For the first time in weeks I have a few moments."

"Thank you, Rolando, but I didn't come here to see you today."

"How will I ever make friends in the U.S. if my writer friends don't tell them about me?"

"Rolando," Dodge said, "with your political leanings it will take a hell of a lot more writers than me to sell you to the American people."

"You can do it, Jack. I trust you."

"Maybe later."

"There's only a few days left." Enrique reminded Dodge.

"Yes, I know, but I have a personal thing to take care of first."

He looked over Enrique's shoulder to the room where Paige was working. She happened to glance up at that moment but quickly went back to her work.

"Excuse me, gentlemen." Dodge moved toward her room.

"Of course." Rolando looked around. "A young woman. What is a presidential candidate compared to that?"

Enrique laughed, then he, Rolando, and the stone-faced Salazar returned to the back room. Dodge walked into Paige's room, stopping in front of her desk, his hands nervously moving around on West's notebook. After a moment, she looked up.

"Hi," Dodge said.

"Hello."

"Are you busy?"

"I have things to do." She unnecessarily reworked some papers, ordering and stacking them neatly.

"Maybe I should come back later?"

"No, it's okay."

"I came by to—uh—apologize."

"You don't have to do that."

"No, I need to. I've—"

"Just a moment." Paige stood up. Dodge watched her like he was afraid she was going to leave, but she only went over and closed the door, then walked back to him. "A little more privacy that way."

"Oh, yeah."

For a moment they stood a foot or so apart looking at each other without saying anything.

"I came to tell you how sorry I am for the way I've behaved toward you," Dodge said. "I've been away so long, I think I've forgotten how to act."

Paige didn't respond, but the beginnings of a smile played around the corners of her mouth.

"I guess what I'm trying to say is, maybe could we start over again? I'll try to be a human being this time, I swear."

"What you are most of all," Paige said, "is human."

"I don't know how to take you."

"Take me the way I am."

"I don't—"

Paige leaned forward and lightly kissed him on the cheek. They looked at each other silently for a moment, then he kissed her softly on the lips.

"We need to talk," he said quietly, "not here."

"Where?"

"I know a place. A beautiful place."

"I need a break anyway." She put her arm around his.

"I just have to drop this off at my place and we can go, okay?" He indicated West's notebook.

"You can leave it here, if you want."

"Think it'll be safe?"

"Sure, I'll lock it up in my desk."

He handed her the notebook and she put it in a top drawer, then locked the desk.

"There you go."

"Let's get out of here." Dodge said.

Arm in arm, they walked out, all eyes in the room on them as they went.

—

The Serrano brothers and Salazar watched Dodge and Paige leave campaign headquarters arms linked together.

"Whooee," Enrique whistled when they were gone, "*Dios mío,* Jack has finally hit the jackpot again."

"*Gringos* are really strange." Rolando said.

"What do you mean?" Salazar asked.

"I mean," Rolando said, "don't they beat all. This lovely girl falls for a *viejo*, an old man, and Dodge—how lucky can one worn out old *gringo* be? It wouldn't surprise me if they weren't a perfect match. He is her rescue project. She is his salvation."

"*Es muy posible,*" Enrique agreed. "Very possible."

"This personal matter is all well and good," Salazar said grimly, "but are they to be trusted so casually?"

"*Sin duda,*" Enrique said, "without doubt."

"The girl is too young not to trust," Rolando said, "as for Jack, I believe he is with us. He always was before."

"I trust him fully," Enrique said. "He's an old friend. Many men drink too much. Unhappiness is not a crime."

"This one," Rolando added, "this girl, maybe she's the one to sober him up."

"Maybe it's all an act with him, the drinking," Salazar suggested.

"No, *compadre*," Rolando dismissed the idea. "He's a real drinker, all right."

"That's for sure," Enrique said. "He's famous at *El Infiernito* and at the *pulqueria* for the amount of tequila he can consume."

"He could be the perfect CIA," Salazar proposed, pronouncing CIA as "seea" in the Spanish style.

"*Dodge?*" Rolando screwed up an eyebrow at Salazar. "Don't be absurd."

"*Absolutamente ridiculo.*" Enrique waved his arms in the air. "Absolutely ridiculous. We've known Jack for many years. Forget this. You're way out of line."

"I only want to protect your candidacy," Salazar protested to Rolando.

Enrique, seemingly tired of Salazar's line, walked to a desk across the room and busied himself with the pretense of going over paperwork. He looked back at Salazar once, and gave the campaign manager a harsh look but Salazar didn't see it or pretended not to.

"I appreciate your concern," Rolando told Salazar, "but, really, Jack Dodge is at best a friend, at worst harmless. Even more so now if he has fallen for the young *gringa*. Perhaps you remember or know what it is like to love a young woman?"

"Of course," Salazar answered in his best macho style.

"Then maybe you can sympathize with our Mr. Dodge?"

"It's not a matter of sympathy, but of campaign security."

"And I appreciate that, Diego, but also remember that Jack Dodge is—or *was*—a famous writer in the U.S. If he is brought back to life by the girl, he may be helpful to our candidacy. He could write good things about us for his press."

"From what I have seen of this *borrachero*, this drunk, it would be quite a *small* press, indeed."

"You underestimate his reputation. If he is rediscovered, it will be a national, perhaps even an international sensation. Maybe you can see the value of such a likelihood."

"Of course, but I think I should still have my brother-in-law with the police—uh—assign someone to him."

"Absolutely not," Rolando said firmly. "Dodge is to be left alone. Am I completely clear?"

"*Sí*," Salazar said, "as you wish. I'll do nothing."

"Good. Now, enough of this, let's get back to work. We have a campaign to finish."

"And a presidency to win," Enrique called over, exchanging a cold look with Salazar.

"*Como no,*" Rolando grinned, "of course."

—

Paige and Dodge were submerged chest high in an outdoor commercial hot spring in the countryside near San Miguel. Behind them were the remains of a sack lunch and two wine bottles, one empty, the other just opened. They passed the newly opened bottle back and forth, their faces flushed from the hot water, the wine, and the excitement of their growing relationship. Dodge, sailing on the crest of a heady wave of personal, nearly forgotten optimism, waxed historical.

"At the time, you know, the lines were clearly drawn. I made my choice. I couldn't allow myself to be pulled in so far, it would have been too great a compromise."

"But it was such a big award."

"It reeked of compromise, of the established order rewarding one of its new literary lions and trying to make him a good little boy. The prospect made me sick."

"Would you do it again?" Paige handed the wine bottle to Dodge. "I mean, given how things have turned out?"

"There are a lot of things I'd do differently." He sipped on the wine. "I think I'm more pragmatic now, more realistic."

"I think you're still a complete idealist."

"I don't feel that way much anymore."

"You've treated yourself badly." She moved next to him.

"Mostly others."

"You mustn't go on punishing yourself for the past."

"Why do you care about me?" He brushed a stray lock of hair out of her eyes. "Like you seem to?"

"It's been a long time for you, hasn't it?"

"Long ago I gave up on the idea of having another meaningful relationship with a woman. What would be the point? Women are always looking for young, cool, good-looking guys. I'm off on all three counts. The only one I ever had was youth."

"I think men are looking for much the same with women." She put her arm around his shoulders. "Not everybody has to have the physically perfect mate. I think you're confusing love and lust."

"Maybe."

"Some people are still looking for other things in a relationship, things like caring, trust, character, experience."

"I've got the experience part all right. Too much of it. Hell, I'm twice your age."

"Not quite and besides, what's that got to do with it?"

"But you're special."

"It took you long enough to notice."

He looked into her deep, smiling eyes, searching for what he didn't know. Rescue, salvation, redemption? He leaned forward and kissed her gently. She kissed him back and then they held each other in a light, sensual embrace. He reached back with his right hand to set the wine bottle down. It swayed briefly and then tipped over, its contents pouring out onto the ground beside the spring. Holding each other tightly, they didn't even notice.

21

Despite his fear, the harsh irony of being sequestered in the House of the Inquisitor was not lost upon Steve, who sat tied up in a cane-backed chair in a dusty side room of the old building. Two of Mendoza's thugs, the ones known to Jack Dodge and Mel West as Shades and Pork Pie, stood close by, ready as usual to deal out physical abuse, which the bruises on Steve's face stood witness to already. Behind and to his left, lurking in a darkened doorway, someone—he couldn't see who—seemed to be signaling orders to the two thugs.

"One more time, *maricón*." Shades looked for direction from the person out of Steve's sight. "Who do you work for?"

Pork Pie punctuated Shade's question with a backhand that drew blood from Steve's nose.

"I already told you." Steve struggled to breathe through the blood. "I'm a student photographer. I take pictures. That's all."

Pork Pie looked past him again. Steve tried to turn in his chair to see who was back there. Shades threatened to hit him. Steve flinched.

"Look this way," Pork Pie ordered.

"You *gringos* make me sick," Shades said. "You are always coming to

Mexico and interfering with us. Mexico is not your concern. You think everything belongs to you. We don't need you here."

"Then let me go. I promise to leave. Honest."

"Honest," Pork Pie mimicked.

"You stuck your nose into our business too far, *puto*," Shades said.

"I haven't done anything."

"You see too much. You'll tell your *comunista* friends."

"You mean that's what this is about? That threat down in Oaxaca? I thought it was just some crank doing it. I thought it didn't matter."

"It matters to you, *maripo*—" Shades cut short his verbal assault at the sound of a rapping on the front door of the house.

Steve tried to cry out but Pork Pie quickly slapped a heavy, fat hand across his mouth and held it there tightly. Shades pulled a short-barreled, small caliber pistol from his pocket, moved into the main room, and slid up next to the front door. The knocking came two or three more times and then it stopped. Steve saw Shades suddenly move to one side as a *gringo* man's face appeared at a side window. It was the man he had passed earlier when he first came to the house. The man tried to see into the darkened building by cupping his hands around the sides of his head to block the outside light.

After a few moments of squinting vainly through the window, the man disappeared. There were another couple of knocks on the front door and then the sound of footsteps going on up the sidewalk. Shades came back into the side room, looked again to the back of the room for instructions, but Steve could tell he didn't receive any.

"Put the tape back on his mouth and check the ropes again." Shades told Pork Pie when he felt sure the gringo had gone.

"Bueno." Pork Pie removed his hand from Steve's mouth.

"My friends will be looking for me." Steve gasped.

"Your friends will think you went back to the United States or died in a whorehouse." Shades said.

Pork Pie joined in the merriment. He seemed to think the part about dying in a whorehouse was particularly funny.

"You'll never get away with this. Nobody will—"

Shades signaled Pork Pie to tape Steve's mouth shut, which he immediately did.

"*Adios, gringo,*" Pork Pie said, with a big, dumb grin. "Don't go anywhere." He and Shades got a real laugh at that.

"We'll be back."

Steve watched the two thugs exit to his left, placing a large *Closed for Repairs* sign on the outside of the door. As soon as they were gone, he bounced wildly around in his chair, trying to yell through the tape over his mouth. In his gyrations, he managed to catch a glimpse of the person who had been signaling orders from the dark to the thugs. Though he couldn't speak the name out loud, it sounded in his head like a cannon going off.

Salazar!

—

Paige sat on the bed in her room at the San Pablo recording her thoughts on a small, hand-held digital recorder. Leaning back against the bedstead with two pillows propped up behind her for support, she had spread some papers on the bed in front of her. A half-empty 7-Up sat on a nightstand beside the bed.

"I'm worried about Steve," she spoke into the recorder, "it's not like him to disappear like this. Especially with the election just around the corner and us so busy. Still, he's a grown boy and can take care of himself. Maybe he just found himself a *señorita.* That would be great. He needs that. What I need is to catch my breath. This thing with JD is moving really fast and maybe it's more than I bargained for. But he does seem to be coming out of his shell rather nicely. He's such a classic drop-out case. He reminds me of Reverend Shannon in *Night of the Iguana* or Rick in *Casablanca.* At least he may start writing again. That would make it all worthwhile, however it works out. As a writer he reminds me of other eccentric, reclusive types like Thomas Pynchon, J.D. Salinger, Ambrose Bierce, and a new one I've heard of down here—B. Traven, the guy who wrote *Treasure of the Sierra Madre.* Sometimes it's all so exciting. I'm really happy I came down. I haven't told JD who I am yet. He just knows me as Paige, but sometimes he'll say something or look at me in a certain way and I think he sees Mom when she was young, but he can't quite place it. I guess I'll have to tell him soon but don't particularly want to. He's so mercurial at times, I don't know how he would react. But I'll have to sooner or later. And speaking of sooner or later." She paused briefly to check her watch. "I've got to run and get some food before I put in more time at Serrano headquarters. This is me signing off for now. Will try to find out about Steve."

She clicked off the recorder and set it on the table by the bed. Grabbing her bag and a couple of the papers she'd been perusing, she hopped up to go. At the door she gave the room a quick once over to make sure she hadn't forgotten anything. Satisfied all was squared away, she pulled the door shut and locked it as she left.

—

Paige busily arranged her bag as she walked up from the San Pablo toward the plaza. Distracted as she was, she turned to the right one street earlier than she had intended. Moments later, Mel West emerged from the next street above, missing Paige by seconds. He turned left onto the street leading away from the plaza and walked downhill toward the San Pablo. He strode the short two and a half blocks to the hotel purposefully and entered through the large front doors.

As usual, the young clerk was working the counter at the San Pablo when West came in. He gave the unkempt *gringo* a once over but put on his professional, if cool, attitude as West walked up to the counter.

"*Sí, señor,* how may I help you?"

"I'm looking for a young girl."

"I'm sorry, sir, we're not that kind of hotel."

"I'm not looking for her for that." West was in no mood for a misunderstanding, intentional or otherwise. "There's a young student journalist staying here. I think she has a friend here, too. A boy, who takes pictures?"

"You wish to see the young lady?" The clerk continued being dense. "Do you know her name?"

"If she's in, yes, I want to see her. Her name's—Paige something, I think, yeah, Paige."

The clerk made a production of looking to see if Paige's key was in the slot for her room.

"I'm sorry, sir, she's out now."

"What about the friend?"

"I believe his name is Steve."

"Whatever. Is he here?" The clerk again looked over at the key slots.

"No, sir. He is out as well."

"I want to leave a message."

"You may if you wish." The clerk rolled his eyes.

"Gee, thanks. You got some paper and a pencil?"

The clerk reluctantly offered a pad of paper and pen. West scribbled off a quick note and handed it to him.

"Be sure the girl gets this."

The clerk grabbed the note and stuffed it in Paige's key slot. West turned and stalked out of the room. The clerk made an obscene gesture at his back. When West was gone, the clerk took the note out of the key slot, looked it over, crumpled it up and tossed it in a nearby waste basket

—

The artist, Bruce, leaned against the mail counter talking to Martha Price when a refreshed looking Jack Dodge entered the door of *El Puente*.

"Well, hello, Mr. Dodge!"

"What'ya say, Bruce, old buddy?"

"Art show at the Institute tonight, Jack. You gonna honor us with your glowing presence this time?"

"Sorry, other plans."

"I guess old friends just don't compare to young women reporters, do we?" Bruce acted offended.

"Geez, this is a small town."

"As small as they get," Martha observed.

"Just the right size, if you get my meaning," Bruce giggled.

"You're incorrigible," Dodge said. "Get out of here with that stuff."

"Well, I do have to run. If you change your mind about the show."

"Thanks, I'll have to take a rain check."

"Suit yourself." Bruce patted Dodge on the shoulder. "Ta ta. Don't take any wooden interviews."

"Break a leg," Dodge told him.

"Be seeing you."

When Bruce had gone, Dodge replaced him at the counter.

"Hi, Jack."

"How are you, Martha?"

"Fine, thanks, you're certainly looking chipper these days."

"Things are going well right now," Dodge admitted.

"I guess she is, I mean I guess they are."

"Is it that well known?"

"Honey," Martha said, "you've said yourself a thousand times how small San Miguel is."

"Yeah, I guess so."

"Say, Jack, old Mr. Hornsby came back yesterday and he found a letter for you in his mail box. Connie thinks she may have put it in there by mistake. Yours is right below his, you know. It's easy to do."

"A letter for me?"

"Here, let me get it." Martha checked his mail box.

"How long has it been there?"

"Check it." Martha handed him the letter.

"For cryin' out loud, what is that, two, three weeks ago it came in?"

"We're sorry, Jack."

"That's okay, it's probably not important anyway."

He opened the letter and read it. Martha commented on his reaction.

"Jack, is there something wrong? Not bad news, I hope."

Dodge didn't speak. It was as if he had suddenly been struck deaf and dumb. After a moment, he turned and without a word walked out of *El Puente.* Behind him, Martha called out a final apology.

"Jack, Jack. We're sorry. We—uh—oh, well. Shoot."

22

Mel West lurked in the shadows of the poorly lit street running behind the House of the Inquisitor. Sneaking up to the backside of the building, he peered in a clear corner of an otherwise darkened window pane. Inside, he could make out an area lit by a single weak light bulb. In that area was the young man he was sure was Steve Thompson, bound to a chair with his mouth taped shut.

Pork Pie and Scar stood behind Steve and in front of him were Shades and, now clearly revealed, Serrano's campaign manager, Diego Salazar. Also beside Salazar was a heavy set middle-aged Mexican man, who West recognized as Mendoza, the local strong man.

"Mendoza! With Salazar." West whistled softly. "Man, this is getting deep."

For a few moments more, he watched the men inside the building seemingly engaged in a heated discussion. Then Mendoza, Salazar, and the three thugs walked toward the back door. West scurried to the safety of a nearby darkened doorway. The men came out the back door.

"No screw-ups." Mendoza told the others as they gathered in the darkness of the deserted street.

"It will be taken care of." Salazar assured the bulky strongman.

"See that it is."

"*Bueno.*"

Mendoza wheeled and walked off, away from where West was hiding.

"Watch him." Salazar signaled Scar to go back into the building. "I'll call you when it's time."

"*Sí, jefe.*" Scar went back inside to keep an eye on Steve.

Outside, Salazar and the other two men walked toward West's hiding place. Just as they got dangerously close to him, a cab rounded the corner and pulled up at a house across the street. A couple and two children got out of the cab, laughing and singing. Salazar and his men turned on their heels and quickly walked away from the taxi's headlights.

"Whoa, baby." West let out a deep breath of air. "That was way too close."

—

Dodge sat at a back table in *La Selva Oscura* drinking when Paige entered the bar. She surveyed the bar, spotted him and hurried over to the table.

"Hello, Mr. Dodge," she said happily. "I was hoping to find you here."

"Here I am." He didn't raise his head.

"What's wrong, Jack? He looked up at her but didn't make eye contact. "What is it?"

"I *knew* you looked familiar."

"So."

"You couldn't tell me? I suppose it would have got in the way of the story."

"What are you talking about?"

"I should have known better. I let myself go. I did know better, you—"

"What's going on?"

He pushed the letter he had received the day before toward her. She frowned, then picked up the letter. It was from her mother.

Dear Jack,

Please forgive the long lapse, but it's serious. My daughter Paige is coming down there to find and write about you. She wants to rediscover and rehabilitate you. She's too young and starstruck with you. For my sake, and for Tom's, and for old times, don't encourage her, please. Remember what it all once meant to us.

For the love we all had,
Sherry Warren.

"You two really cared about each other once, didn't you?" Paige laid the letter on the table.

"That's not the point and you know it."

"When did this come?"

"Does that matter?"

"When?"

"A couple of weeks ago, I don't know. It was lost and I just got it yesterday." He looked at Paige as if expecting some kind of response. It was not voluntarily forthcoming. "Well?"

"Well, what?"

"What about this?" He tapped the letter.

"Maternal protectiveness, what else?"

"You know you should have told me who you are."

"How could it possibly matter that I'm—"

"How could it matter that you're the daughter of some of my best and oldest friends?"

"Don't be upset."

"How can I not be? You're young enough to be *my* daughter. Hell, you really could *be* my daughter."

"That's bull, I'm not and you know it. That's mean to my mom and dad."

"Mean? Damn it, girl, you got a skewed idea of what's mean, I'd say."

"And you've been hiding from life so long that you've forgotten what has meaning and what doesn't. Of all people, Jack, you should know that our ages and who we are is completely irrelevant. It's how we feel about each other that matters. It's all that matters."

"If it's all that matters, then what's all that about rehabilitating me and writing about me?"

"Those are my mother's words."

"Did you come down here just to get a story on me or what?"

"Don't yell."

"I'm not yelling." A few people in the bar looked over at them.

"If you can't tell that what's going on between us is more than a story for me," Paige lowered her voice, "then you've lost more than I thought you had."

"What's that supposed to mean?"

"What it means is that it's my turn to walk away, Jack, and I'm going right now. I promise not to write a single word about you. You can stay here and wallow in alcohol and self-pity if you want. I'm going to Mexico City to cover election day and that's that."

"I—"

"We'll all be staying at the Majestic Hotel by the *zocalo*." She stood to go. "If you decide to rejoin the human race, the world you think you know so well may be changing there in a couple of days. You might not want to miss it."

Without waiting for a response, she turned and walked away, out of the bar, out into the pleasant San Miguel evening. Stunned, Dodge sat at his table unmoving, unable to stop her, silently watching her go.

—

Emma was behind the bar at *El Infiernito* when Mel West barged in.

"What an honor for you to grace my poor *cantina*, did you get tired of the life uptown?"

"What are you talking about? I came to see if—"

"Now that the young *gringa* is in town, my main customers no longer come. I can see you are under her spell, too. I didn't think you were foolish like that."

"For cryin' out loud, Emma, gimme a break. I got bigger fish to fry than just that new girl. But I *am* looking for her and Dodge. It's urgent. Have you seen them?"

"They wouldn't come to a place like this."

"My, God, you're *jealous*. I can't believe it. After all the time you've known Dodge."

Emma grabbed a bar towel and began to wipe several glasses that were already clean.

"Look, you know Jack as well as I do. Maybe this girl could be the best thing for him. Who knows? Maybe she'll get him writing again. Besides, I thought you liked her."

"I *do* like her, that's why it's worse."

"Well, listen, let that stuff go for now. I'm onto something and I can't find either one of them. The kid that was with the girl is in big trouble."

"I never even knew there was someone else with her."

"Neither did I till lately, but something is up. And big."

"What do you mean? Big like what?"

"Big like Mendoza."

"I'm telling you now, Mel, if it's Mendoza, stay out of it—whatever it is."

"It may concern Rolando, too."

"Politics." She waved her arms around. "Please don't get involved. And don't get Jack and the girl into it either. Stay clear."

"I don't think I can."

"I don't want to hear any more." She turned away.

"You don't know where they are, then?"

"No." She refused to look at West. "I haven't seen either of them for days."

"Then I'm going to have to do it myself."

"Mel, don't." Emma turned back to face him. "Please don't get yourself hurt. It's not worth it."

"Don't worry, I'm too big a coward to get myself hurt but I have to do something."

"You stupid, stubborn men."

"It does seem to run in the gender, I guess. Save me a shot of tequila?"

"Nothing but grown up boys."

"*Nos vemos.*" West headed for the door. "See you later."

"*Que te vayas bien, chico.*" Emma said to the empty bar when West had gone. "Good luck."

—

Dodge laid Sherry Warren's letter on the counter of one of three phone booths in a little telephone service kiosk on a side street in San Miguel. He was placing a call to the states and after a surprisingly short time, the call went through to *The New Populist.*

"Can I speak to Ben Michaels, please? Jack Dodge. Yes, that's right, Jack Dodge, from Mexico. Thanks. Hello. Ben, I'm sure glad you're still there. It's Jack Dodge from San Miguel. I'm glad to talk to you again, too. Yes, I'm aware of the presidential elections. I'm getting ready to go there right now. Sounds great. Oh, don't worry about that, we can arrange it when I come up next time."

Dodge picked up the letter from Sherry Warren and held it where he could see it while he continued talking. After a moment, he wadded up the letter and pitched it into a trash can just outside the phone booth.

"You bet," he told the editor on the other end of the line. "I'm ready to go."

23

The glass front doors of the Hotel Majestic were getting quite a workout. People, mostly reporters, came in from and went out to Avenue Madero which led directly into Mexico City's grandiose central plaza, the *zocalo*. The area was in a frenzy of pre-election activity and many interested parties stayed at the Majestic to get a close up view of the process.

Among a noisy group returning to the Majestic late in the afternoon were Paige, Jean Holland, and several Serrano campaign workers. Andres had stayed behind at the hotel in the hope that Steve would somehow show up. The incoming group brimmed with excitement as the intensity and significance of the elections, now only a day away, began to build perceptibly. Paige was flushed and talkative as the group reached the counter to collect their room keys.

"This is so incredible. I'm so glad I came."

"And your stories are getting out, too," Jean said. "You're getting some space in the international press."

"That's wonderful." Paige said joyfully.

Her mood quickly turned somber when she saw Andres get off the elevator and walk toward the counter.

"Andres, still no word?"

"Nothing yet. No one knows anything, I am a little worried also."

"Because of what happened in Oaxaca?"

"*Sí, señorita*, especially because of Oaxaca."

"How long's it been?" Jean said.

"Several days."

"Did anyone think to call the police?"

"I talked to my cousin in the army up in San Miguel," Andres said. "He is checking for me. But so far nothing."

"I keep hoping he'll just show up," Paige said. "He's missing such an amazing thing here."

"You really like this, don't you?" Jean said.

"I love it. I just wish we knew where Steve was."

"Has anyone tried his phone?"

"Of course, but the service has been so erratic we kind of gave up on that. I don't think it was turned on anyway."

"I'm sure he'll be all right."

"Yes, I'm sure, too," Andres echoed.

"I hope you're right," Paige said.

"You'll see," Andres told her. "He'll show up. He'll be okay."

A middle-aged skinny clerk, who had been busy while the threesome talked to one another in front of the counter, handed Paige her key without waiting for her request. "Here you are, Miss," he said. "Number 348."

"Thank you. Do I have any messages?"

"*Momentito*," the clerk checked behind the desk. "I'm sorry, *señorita*, there is nothing."

"If anything comes for me, will you please let me know right away?"

"Of course, right away, I will."

"Thank you."

"We've got to go back to the paper for a while," Jean said, when Paige's attention was back on her and Andres, "but we'll be back here later. Would you like to meet us for supper at Sanborn's?"

"I'm going to try to settle down a little first. Maybe we could call San Miguel again also?"

"We will," Andres assured her.

"Thank you."

"It's okay."

"Then perhaps later?" Jean said.

"Maybe so," Paige said, "now I just want to unwind a little."

"Okay. I understand. We'll see you after a while."

"See you guys."

Paige headed for the elevator.

"*Ciao,*" Jean waved goodbye.

"*Nos vemos*," Andres added.

With a wave, Paige turned and entered the elevator.

—

Paige finished showering and sat down on the edge of the hotel bed to dry her hair with a large towel. She wore jogging shorts and a T-shirt that was wet around the shoulders from her hair. As she was towel-drying her hair, there was a knock on the door. She brushed the hair back out of her eyes with her hands.

"Who is it?"

"Room service." She recognized the voice of the skinny desk clerk.

"Just a minute."

Draping the towel over her shoulders, she went to the door and opened it part way. To her complete surprise, the skinny clerk was standing behind a cart upon which lay a dozen red roses, a bowl of fresh fruit, and a bucket of champagne.

"*Buenas tardes, señorita.*" The clerk smiled, revealing a row of healthy but crooked teeth.

"*Buenas tardes*." She cocked an eye at the cart.

"These are for you."

"For me? Wonderful, but I didn't—"

Before she could finish her sentence, Jack Dodge suddenly appeared from behind the door, smiling and looking as happy as she had ever seen him.

"But I did," he said.

"Jack!" Paige rushed to him, gave him a big hug.

The clerk scratched his chin and looked away. After the hug and a quick kiss, Dodge pulled back, reached into his jacket pocket and produced a tip for the clerk.

"*Gracias, señor, algo mas?*"

"*No, gracias. Quizas mas tarde.* Maybe later."

"*Muy bien.*"

With a satisfied look at his tip and a high sign for Dodge, the clerk walked away whistling. Laughing, Dodge and Paige pushed the cart into the room and closed the door behind.

—

Dodge and Paige leaned back into pillows propped against the headboard of her bed, sipping what little remained of the champagne he had brought. They sat close together, occasionally touching as they casually chatted.

"It's so great that you're going to write again."

"Well, it's just for these last couple of days of the election. No promises yet for the future."

"Still." Paige savored a strawberry with a small drink of champagne.

"*The New Populist* was really good to me. They seemed happy to have me do it."

"Why wouldn't they? You know you still have a reputation in the States. Some progressive professors even teach your books."

"They do?"

"Yes. I've been trying to tell you that ever since we met."

"I'll be damned."

"You still have a lot to say, Jack."

He leaned over and kissed her on the cheek.

"And you're about the sweetest girl I've ever known. She took his hand in hers and they linked fingers. "Thank you."

"For what?"

"For giving me my life back."

"I didn't do that. You did it."

"You helped me find it then."

Of a sudden, Paige's smile faded. Dodge saw.

"What?"

"My friend Steve—"

"Oh, heck. Still no word?"

"None.

"I'm sorry. I've been so carried away with my own life, with you, that I— when did you last see him?"

"It's been several days. I'm getting scared about it."

"Does he do this kind of thing often?"

"Oh, no, not Steve. He's Mr. Dependable."

"Maybe he found himself a girlfriend?"

"That's what I hoped, but it's been too long. There's something wrong."

"Well as soon as we get a chance tomorrow." He promised. "I'll call Mel in San Miguel and see if he knows anything. Okay?"

"Okay."

Dodge ran his fingers through her hair. She looked at him and smiled. He kissed her softly on the lips.

"As soon as we get a chance," she said.

"As soon as."

Taking their champagne glasses, Dodge set them on the tray by the bed. Pulling back the covers, he reached for her and they slid back down into the bed and held onto each other tightly.

24

In the first light of dawn, Mel West worked to pry open a door at the back of the historic House of the Inquisitor. Pushing aside a *Closed for Repairs* sign, he managed to dislodge the door and then cautiously opened it. After a careful look around, he entered the building and closed the door behind.

He slowly moved forward. In the interior of the building, he spotted Steve Thompson, still tied to a chair with his mouth taped shut. Across the room he saw Scar dozing in a chair with his back to the wall.

Scrounging around for a weapon, he found a short two by four in a pile of scrap lumber. Steve glanced up just then and though West knew the boy didn't know who he was, he saw hope flash in the young captive's eyes.

He signaled with his free hand for Steve to remain still and began to sneak up on the thug. He was almost to the man when he tripped against an unseen bucket, sending it rattling across the room. Startled awake, Scar went for his pistol as he rose.

West quickly recovered and with a swiftness he didn't know he was capable of brought the two by four down across the side of the rising thug's head.

With a grunt, Scar dropped to the floor nearly unconscious. West stared in amazement until the guy tried to get to his feet, then hit him again—hard. That did it. Scar was down and out. For a moment, West stood over him, stunned by his success. Then he did a little jig around the fallen tough.

"You're outta here." He swung the two by four back and forth like a baseball bat. "Home run." Steve's muffled cries brought West back to earth.

"Hey, bud. I bet you're glad to see me." Steve banged up and down in the chair. "Oh, here, let me get you loose."

West dropped the two by four and started untying Steve who grunted more frantically. It occurred to him that he should take the tape off Steve's mouth and he did so rather roughly.

"Ow! Are you rescuing me or trying to hurt me worse?"

"Sorry, pal."

"Who are you?"

"West's the name, Mel West. This is a rescue. You can thank me later."

"Thanks," Steve said when he was untied.

He creakily stood up and, groaning, stretched his knotted, tired muscles.

"Think nothing of it," West said cavalierly. "What did you do to get Mendoza, Salazar, and their cronies to lock you up in the House of the Inquisitor? Nice irony, huh?"

"Yeah, real ironic. I was laughing the whole time."

"I bet you were. They're real funny guys."

"I can't believe it was Salazar, too. Mr. Serrano's own campaign manager."

"Pretty slimy, huh?"

"That bastard," Steve said. "Listen, we've got to get a hold of Serrano's people right away."

"Your friend, the girl. She's with Serrano's people in Mexico City. Maybe we can reach her there."

"Right." Steve rubbed his sore wrists. "I think I know where they'll be staying. Where can we send an email or call from?"

"*El Puente* will be opening soon," West looked at his watch. "We can do it from there."

"Excellent, now let's get outta this joint."

"Grab that jerk's gun." West pointed at Scar who was beginning to stir again. Steve carefully picked up the gun.

"What do we do about him?"

West picked up the two by four, spit on each hand, adjusted his grip and then blasted the thug in the head again. The man crumpled to the floor.

"That's for taking my notebook, punk," West said to the motionless body.

"C'mon, hurry. We've gotta get word to Paige."

"Take off." West pointed to the back door.

Hustling outside, the two men turned left and raced on in the direction of *El Puente.*

25

On the day before the national elections, Mexico City's *zocalo* was packed with an excited, boisterous, and mobile crowd numbering in the many thousands. Streamers, balloons, and political signs of every size, shape, and point of view cluttered the space above the concrete floor of the central plaza.

At the center of it all was a large stage upon which Rolando Serrano stood delivering his final campaign speech. In the midst of the large throng that alternately cheered and listened intently, Dodge and Paige wound their way toward the platform. They eventually stopped a few yards away where they commanded a relatively unobstructed view of the proceedings.

On Rolando's right on stage was his brother Enrique and to his left, Diego Salazar. Dodge and Paige busied themselves taking notes and she held up a small mic trying to catch some of Rolando's comments. Unnoticed by either of them, a young reporter stood close by frequently eyeing Dodge. He saw Paige, yielding to impulse, lean over and kiss Dodge on the cheek.

"Incredible, isn't it, Jack?" she said above the crowd noise.

Hearing the name 'Jack', the young reporter sidled closer yet. Dodge saw him, but was too excited to care.

"I haven't been this fired up in years."

"Welcome back to the world, Jack Dodge," Paige said happily.

"Right on."

The young reporter jotted rapidly in his notebook and could hardly hide a triumphant look. In their excitement and self-concentration, Jack and Paige didn't even notice.

—

The main clerk behind the counter at the Majestic was thumbing through a pile of mail and papers when he happened upon a note addressed to Paige Warren. Recognizing the name as belonging to the young *gringa*, he pulled it from the other papers and held it up to the light to examine it more closely.

"*Ay, Díos mío!*" He saw "Urgent" marked on the outside of the note. He frantically waved it at the skinny clerk who was just coming out of a back room into the main hallway of the hotel. "*Mira, mira. Ven*. Look, come here." The other clerk hurried over.

"*Qué pasa?* What's going on?"

"This message got mixed up with some other papers. It's marked urgent for the young *señorita*. Warren. The one with the older *gringo* man."

"*Sí, sí,*" the skinny clerk said. "*Señor* Dodge."

"Yes."

"*Ay*, but they are out in the *zocalo* already." The skinny clerk put his right hand on top of his head.

"I know. Take this to them, anyway, now."

"In all that crowd? I might not find them."

"You have to try. This says urgent. Here. Hurry."

"*Muy bien*. I'll try."

"Hurry, *vaya*."

The skinny clerk rushed out the door and headed directly for the *zocalo*.

—

As Rolando Serrano's rousing speech went on, Paige and Dodge managed to get even closer to the speaker's platform where they stood side by side. As Serrano discussed land reform to the adoring crowd, Diego Salazar began to edge away to the left of the candidate.

The movement caught Dodge's eye and he followed Salazar's movements and then saw him nod to someone nearby in the crowd. He traced Salazar's line of sight and was surprised to see the tough guy he and Mel West called Shades standing by the base of the platform off to the right. He slipped in behind Paige so that Shades couldn't see him. She thought he was being playful.

"What are you doing back there?"

"Something's not right about this."

His tone made her turn back around where she unsuccessfully scrutinized the crowd for signs of trouble. He pressed her shoulder to make her look back at the stage.

"Do you see something?"

"There's something funny going on here. What's Salazar doing signaling to one of Mendoza's goons?"

"Mendoza, the political boss? Is he here somewhere?"

Before he could explain, he heard his name being called from behind. He turned around and saw the skinny clerk picking his way through the crowd toward them.

"*Señor* Dodge! *Señor* Dodge!"

To avoid being seen by Shades or noticed by Salazar, Dodge ducked back into the crowd, pulling Paige along with him. They were soon joined by the clerk. The young reporter who had been watching them tried to get within earshot.

"*Señor* Dodge! *Señorita* Warren!" the clerk gasped. "I'm so lucky I found you. This message came for you. It is urgent."

They took the note and quickly read it together.

"Mel rescued your pal Steve," Dodge cried out loud, "and they're on their way down here."

"And look," Paige said, "it says Salazar and Mendoza are in on something against Rolando. Maybe a hit. Oh my gosh, Jack. We've got to do some…."

Before she could finish her sentence, he was already shoving his way toward the speaker's platform. She stuffed the note in her bag and charged after him. The uncomprehending clerk watched them go. The young reporter chased along behind.

Struggling through the crowd, Dodge finally emerged just a few feet from the front of the platform. As he did, he looked up to see Salazar pointing and yelling at him. Before he could warn the Serrano people, Salazar leaped forward on the podium brandishing a Mexican flag that had been strategically placed to one side.

"*¡Viva Mexico!*" he yelled out. "*¡Viva! ¡Viva!*"

At these words, Shades pulled a long barrel .38 revolver from inside his coat. He clambered onto the stage and rushed the podium, the weapon pointed at Rolando Serrano. Caught completely off guard, the Serrano people momentarily froze, exactly what Shades needed for a clear shot.

With a cry, he aimed the weapon at Serrano's chest and was about to squeeze the trigger when Dodge clambered onto the platform and threw himself at the hit man. The .38 discharged with a loud crack and Enrique Serrano dropped to the floor of the stage just to the right of where Dodge and the would-be assassin struggled for control of the pistol.

In the ensuing mayhem, Paige and the crowd watched in horror as Rolando briefly knelt beside his wounded brother, then in a red-eyed rage rushed Salazar. The two men struggled fiercely. Salazar fought with the sharp end of the flagpole but Rolando managed to land a powerful roundhouse right that knocked his assailant down.

Salazar fell into Dodge and Shades and the collision sent the .38 skidding across the stage. Dodge was getting the worst of the exchange, but with the crowd surging forward and Serrano's people reacting, Shades and Salazar were forced to make a run for it.

They bolted to the edge of the stage but were pushed back by the angry pro-Serrano crowd, which held them in check until a small detachment of

Mexico City police burst through and surrounded them. The police also detained Dodge, but Rolando Serrano hurriedly came to his aid.

"*Déjense,*" he ordered the police, "let him go. He's one of my people. He's with us."

The police released Dodge, and he and Rolando stood triumphantly at center stage. The crowd roared and cheered.

"Those are the two you're after." Rolando indicated Salazar and Shades to the police. "Get them out of here."

The worked up crowd let out another big roar as the police hauled Salazar and Shades away. Paige slipped through the commotion and when Dodge saw her he helped her up onto the stage. Rolando gave both of them bear hugs.

"My old friend," he said emotionally to Dodge, "you saved our lives. And you young lady, thank you."

"How is Enrique?" Dodge looked behind them.

"It did not look bad," Rolando said, "but it was close enough."

"Look," Paige said, as Enrique, holding his slightly wounded left arm, walked across the stage toward them, "here he is."

"*Aqui,*" Enrique said with a pained smile, "here I am. I'm okay. I don't think the arm is broken even. I am lucky he was a bad shot."

"Thanks to Jack." Rolando clasped Dodge on the shoulder with his right hand. "How can we ever thank you? You are truly a friend."

"Just win this election, Rolando. Make Mexico proud."

"We will. We will."

The two men hugged again and shook hands, then Rolando turned to tend to his brother. Paige fussed over Dodge's bruised face.

"When I told you to get involved again, I didn't mean get yourself killed."

He took her hands away from his face and held them, then he kissed her, long and ardently. The still buzzing crowd nearby let out a cheer, led by the skinny clerk who hooted loudly.

In the background, hardly noticed, the sirens of approaching police and medical vehicles blared. Close by, also unnoticed, the young reporter stood to one side rapidly taking notes.

26

Late in the morning on election day, Dodge, Paige, and Jean Holland went for coffee at an outdoor café just around the corner from the Majestic Hotel. Dodge faced the now quiet *zocalo* with Jean across the table from him and Paige on his left.

At a table to Jean's right sat the ubiquitous young reporter from the previous day. He was also having coffee and trying not to make it too obvious that he was watching Dodge. For his part, Dodge acted like he didn't see the young reporter and instead kept looking back in the direction of the hotel.

"What's keeping Andres? The papers must have come in by now."

"Maybe they're late." Jean winked at Paige. "Typical, you know."

"I thought you didn't like the limelight, Jack?" Paige teased.

"I guess I am getting a little carried away, huh?"

"You have the right to, if you ask me," Jean said.

"I like you a lot better this way." Paige put her hand on Dodge's arm.

"Oh, here he comes."

Jean waved to Andres who came around the corner toward them with an armload of newspapers.

"Wow." Paige admired the stack of papers. "You got them all."

"I had to go to the Ritz," Andres explained, "the Majestic didn't get their delivery yet." He tossed the papers down on the table and the group greedily poured over them.

"Front page of the *Times*, of course," Paige noted.

"Uh-huh," Jean said, "front page in *La Prensa*, too. Congratulations."

"Excellent," Dodge said. "What did the *Times* say?"

"Listen to this," Jean read. "*A man believed to be reclusive American writer, Jack Dodge, foiled an assassination attempt against Mexican presidential candidate Rolando Serrano yesterday in Mexico City. The man wrestled with the assailant, knocking a high-powered handgun out of the as yet unidentified Mexican male's hand.*"

"I'd say you've managed to come back with a bang, Mr. Dodge," Paige punned, "so to speak."

Dodge leaned over and kissed her on the cheek.

"Thanks to you, Ms. Warren."

As they went back to reading the papers, a taxi pulled up to the curb a few yards to their right and two men got out.

"*Mira*," Andres cried out, "it's Steve."

"And my old buddy, Mel!"

Dodge jumped up to greet his scrawny friend. Paige raced over to Steve, hugging him so energetically she almost knocked him down.

"Whoa." he looked past her to Jean. "I guess I should get kidnapped every day."

"I was so worried about you. Don't you ever do anything like that again, you hear me?"

"Yes, Momma Warren."

"Oh, my gosh," Paige said, "speaking of Momma Warren, she'll kill us when she reads about this."

"Maybe she won't see it," Dodge suggested. "Maybe it won't be covered by the Denver and Boulder papers."

"That's not too likely," Jean said, "based on what we're seeing, everybody's picking it up."

"Well, I don't care too much about that right now, anyway," Steve said, "and I'll tell you, if it wasn't for Mel here, I don't know what would have happened to me. There might not be a Steve for anybody to be mad at."

"You're both so brave," Paige said. "We're so proud of you."

"Very proud." Jean moved in to give Steve a big hug.

Paige glanced at Dodge but he just raised his eyebrows.

"Looks like we finally did something worthwhile, huh, partner?" West said.

"Took us long enough. Did you get things straightened out in San Miguel before you left?"

"Yeah, seems so. Everybody's been nailed, except Mendoza, of course."

"He'll go one of these times."

"They still might get him this time. If we're lucky."

"You bet." Dodge then regarded Steve. "And this is the Steve I've heard so much about but never seen?"

"I guess you must be Mr. Dodge." Steve offered his hand.

"Call me Jack." Dodge shook his hand. "It's good to finally meet you."

"Same here, it's been an amazing few weeks."

"These internships are getting wilder all the time." Jean said.

"I'd say they must be." Steve made eye contact with her. "But maybe they're worth it."

"We're glad to have you back."

"I could be convinced to stay a little longer."

"We'll have to see about that, perhaps—"

"Excuse me," Paige interrupted, "we need one more introduction. Mel West, this is Jean Holland of *The Times*."

"Nice to meet you."

"My pleasure." Jean said.

"Well, come on everybody," Dodge said happily, "let's sit down and finish breakfast. We were just going over all the papers to see if our story got front page coverage."

"Mr. West," Jean said, "I think you may have a heck of a story to tell also."

She settled into a chair by Steve. Dodge and Andres got a couple more chairs from a nearby table to accommodate the expanding group.

"Not me." West patted Dodge on the shoulder. "I'll leave the fame up to my buddy, here."

"I believe this belongs to you, sir." Paige reached into her bag and pulled out West's notebook.

"Where did you get this?"

"From that sleazebucket Salazar," Dodge said. "If I'd thought about it at the time, it was an obvious tip off to all this."

"If you don't mind my asking," Paige said, "what's in the notebook, Mel?"

"I don't mind. It's everything this Dodge character's been up to for the past few years. I figured someday he might want to write about it and wouldn't recall it all too well."

"You crazy old fart," Dodge said.

"What about the Serranos?" Steve said. "What happened to them?"

"Fortunately, Enrique only had a minor wound," Jean told him. "He was bandaged up and released. And the last minute polls showed Rolando taking the lead in the election."

"Wow." Steve whistled. "Mexican history in the making."

"It is an exciting time for our country," Andres said.

"Why don't we check a few polling places close by and then go have a 'Free Again' celebration somewhere?" Steve suggested. "I need to unwind a little bit."

"Sounds wonderful to me," Jean said.

"Okay," Dodge agreed, "we can read these stories anytime."

"I know just the place in the Zona Rosa," Jean told them.

Collecting all the papers, the happy group rose to leave. Dodge tossed some *pesos* down to cover the coffee and was about to walk away when the young reporter from the nearby table stepped up beside him.

"Excuse me, sir."

"Yes?" Dodge eyed him warily as the others walked away.

"Sir, are you Jack Dodge? The writer?"

"I am Jack Dodge, and I have written."

"Outstanding. Well, sir, I'm Jason Smith from the *Los Angeles Times.* I've been down here covering the elections. I saw everything you did yesterday. Could we talk for a moment?"

"I don't know." Dodge stopped and looked at Paige, who had paused with the others a few yards away. "We were just leaving."

"Please, sir, people are going to want to hear about you. You're news again, big news."

Dodge again looked at Paige.

"Go for it. We'll wait in the Majestic for you. It's your hour, Jack."

"Thank you, Paige."

"My pleasure."

Taking a deep breath, Dodge sat back down at the table. The young reporter took out a digital recorder and a notebook and pen and sat down next to him. "The first thing I have to ask you, Mr. Dodge, is something that people have wanted to know for a long time. Why did you turn down that Pulitzer Prize?"

Dodge glanced over his shoulder at Paige and the others who walked away laughing. They waved as they went. Dodge returned the wave, then turned back to the young reporter.

"I'll tell you, young man," he said with sober confidence, "times were a lot different back then. The country was polarized, the battle lines were drawn, a man had to take a stand...."

YUCATAN DAWN

With dusk settling over Mexico City, John Pastor took in the patchwork of light and shadow playing across the expansive slab of concrete that is the *zocalo*. From his vantage point in the outdoor rooftop café of the Hotel *El Parador*, Pastor had a full, panoramic view of the city's massive downtown square. Directly across the huge plaza from *El Parador* was the national palace, seat of the Mexican government, its interior walls covered in radical Diego Rivera murals.

Further over from the national palace, to the left from his perspective at *El Parador*, Pastor noted the ruins of Tenochtitlan, the Aztec capitol upon which Mexico City was built. The Templo Mayor, the sacrificial pyramid and altar, jutted menacingly up from the edge of the concrete plaza toward the darkening sky in harsh reminder of the untold thousands of indigenous people whose hearts were torn from their living bodies to keep the sun revolving in the Aztec sky.

Shifting his gaze to the nearer left foreground, Pastor took in the massive, lumpy metropolitan cathedral, leaning slightly leeward in deference to the several powerful earthquakes that have shaken the great city over the years.

Built upon the dried remains of Lake Texcoco, Mexico City—perhaps the world's largest city and even more likely its most polluted—is a daily reminder of both the complete destruction of native cultures by sixteenth-century conquistadors and colonialists and of one of the great ecological disasters of modern times. Where once native peoples rowed boats across reed strewn waters, now millions of citizens crisscross untold miles of concrete in car, taxi, bus, and on foot.

Beneath *El Parador,* out of Pastor's viewpoint from the roof, a wide pedestrian-filled sidewalk brimmed with a row of ground level gift shops and small outdoor cafes standing under several stories of office and hotel room windows facing the busy *zocalo.* And directly across from the ground floors, in the center of the quadrangular plaza, Pastor watched as a Mexican army honor guard lowered a gigantic Mexican flag in a patriotic ritual performed at each day's end.

Four beer bottles sat on Pastor's table in the nearly empty restaurant. The ex-border patrolman, now barely making a living as an international private eye in Mexico City, finished the final bite of his meal. Fortyish, with receding light hair, Pastor was tall and fit, one of those aging men, perhaps once handsome, who are often cited as being ruggedly good looking.

Pushing his plate toward the center of the table, Pastor picked up a beer bottle from among the four, checked it out and then downed the last of its contents. Setting it down, he signaled to an attentive waiter, who hurried over to the table.

"*Sí, Señor* Pastor?"

Pastor dug out his wallet, produced two large denomination *peso* bills and handed them to the waiter. Pastor left the billfold open on the table for a moment looking at a picture of himself when he was younger. In the picture with him were a woman and a young girl.

"*Su familia?*" The waiter glanced at the photograph.

"Yes, Carlos." Pastor closed the billfold. "My family."

"They come visit you?"

"No." Pastor frowned. "No visit."

"Oh, I'm sorry, *señor.* I—"

"It's okay." Pastor pocketed the billfold. "Long ago. In the past."

"*Discúlpame*," Carlos said. "Forgive me. I didn't mean to pry."

"Would you bring me some cigarettes and the bill, Carlos, *por favor?*"

"Of course, *señor, pero*... I didn't know you smoked, Mr. Pastor."

"I don't."

"I see." Carlos gave Pastor a funny look.

While Carlos headed toward the cashier at the front of the restaurant, Pastor again gazed at the photo in his billfold. He lingered on it, running his thumb and forefinger over the image of the woman and girl. After a moment, Carlos returned with the cigarettes and Pastor's change. Pastor took the smokes but didn't open them. He placed some coins on the table, then closed his billfold and placed it in an inside coat pocket.

"*Muchas gracias,* Carlos," he said, rising. "*Hasta luego*."

"*Buenas tardes, Señor* Pastor." Carlos said. "See you again soon."

"You bet."

Pastor walked back through the restaurant, nodding to the cashier on his way out. Head down, he crossed an outer hallway to a staircase and descended three flights to the hallway leading to his room. The hallway was poorly lit and quiet, the tread of Pastor's shoes on the hardwood floor the only sound.

Reaching his room, Pastor fished a key out of his pants pocket and opened the door. The room was dark and he paused a moment before he pushed the door shut. With a sigh, he flipped the switch on the overhead room light and was puzzled to hear a similar click emanating from somewhere behind him in the room.

He turned to find himself, for just the third time in his professional career, looking down the barrel of a gun. A short-barreled, silver blue .38 revolver. Fear coated his tongue like a blanket of sour copper dust.

His assailant, a thick, hulking man, seemed as afraid as Pastor was. The men, surprised—perhaps angry at their inability to react quickly—were temporarily motionless. Pastor came out of it first.

He feinted left, then dove across the room to his right, pulling his own weapon, a .380 automatic. As he crashed onto the thinly carpeted floor, the assailant's .38 round whistling by his left shoulder to thud into the cheaply papered hotel wall behind him, Pastor managed to fire a wild, lucky shot. It hit the big man directly in the right knee, felling him like a redwood with a sudden terminal case of tree rot.

Pastor scrambled to his feet and rushed his assailant, who lay on the floor crying and writhing in pain. Blood pumped from his shattered knee.

"Who in the hell are you?" Pastor kicked the .38 across the floor away from the big man.

When the man didn't respond, Pastor moved up next to him and nudged the barrel of his .380 alongside the man's thick, broad cheekbone.

"Come on, son of a bitch."

The man groaned and rolled toward Pastor. Pastor drew back his foot and aimed it at the blasted out knee.

"No, please, mister. No."

"Then talk, pal."

"Help me." Moaning steadily, the man tried to get up. "Help me."

Pastor helped him up and pushed him into a chair by the bed. The big man filled the chair, blood still pumping from his leg.

"Take your tie off," Pastor said, "wrap it around your leg. You're gonna need a doctor."

The man did as he was told and leaned back, faint, in the chair. Pastor brought him a glass of water.

"Thanks, mister."

"Talk," Pastor demanded. "What are you doing in Mexico City and what are you doing drawing down on me like some two-bit gunslinger? The *Federales* ain't gonna like this one bit. Especially when they see it's two *gringos*."

"We gotta get outta here."

"Correction." Pastor said. "I gotta get outta here. You're going to tell me fast what the hell you're doing here and then you're going to deal with the *Policia*. I'll be history."

"You can't do that to me, mister, please."

"Talk fast. Gimme names. Reasons. You got maybe twenty seconds."

"What if I don't?"

"Then the *Federales* find a corpse." Pastor put the .380 against the man's temple. "It's all the same to me."

"Boston," the man said.

"Boston? I don't know anybody in Boston."

"No, Mr. Francis Boston. From Phoenix."

"Sonny Boston?" Pastor said. "The developer? The one busted a couple of years ago for land swindling?"

"Yeah."

"Why me? Why would he be concerned about me finding a missing—"

Pastor stopped in mid-sentence. The man looked up at him fearfully.

"I don't know, mister. I just got the message to do the job."

Pastor cocked his head to the right. Police sirens sounded out in the city somewhere nearby. He put the muzzle of the .380 beneath the man's left eye.

"Make a choice, death or the *Federales*. Give me a local name."

"Jo... Jo *something*. I don't remember."

"Remember." Pastor engaged, then disengaged the safety of his .380.

"Matanza, I think. Yeah, José Matanza."

"Matanza," Pastor's eyes went flat, "and Boston, together here?" He paused, spoke then as much to himself as to his assailant. "Mexican mafia. That figures, slimy bastards. Why would they...."

"I don't know nothin' about that," the big man insisted.

"Huh? Ah, forget it." Pastor walked to the door. "Boston and Matanza must be hard up to send a rookie like you out on a job."

"Can't ever'body be good at stuff," the big man said.

"You got a point there, buddy." Pastor stepped into the hallway and allowed himself a cold laugh.

—

A pale, crescent moon put out little light as Pastor tapped an ornate metal knocker on the front door of an opulent, Spanish-style, white stucco house. It was much quieter in the suburbs of Mexico City than in the heart of the metropolis itself and so he could hear sounds coming from within the house. Looking up, he saw that a camera was mounted above the door and that it was trained directly at him. He winked at the camera just as the door was opened by a young woman.

"*Buenas noches.*" Pastor restrained a whistle.

"*Buenas noches, señor.*" The young woman looked away shyly.

"*Esta en casa, Señor Morales?*"

"*Si, señor. Y su nombre?*"

"John Pastor. I'm a friend."

"Very well, sir."

The girl reentered the house, closing the door behind her but in just moments it opened again and a thin, rough-looking man, openly wearing a pistol holstered at his side appeared. When he saw Pastor, a wide-grin softened his tough features.

"Well, *dios mio*, it's my old friend John Pastor." The man grabbed Pastor and gave him a big hug.

"Chango Morales," Pastor said, "or should I say *Señor* Ephraim Morales, retired head of vice."

"I can still find the vice." Chango laughed loudly. "It's so wonderful to see you again."

"It's good to see you, too."

Chango opened his arms and the old friends embraced warmly.

"Please, come in." Chango kept an arm around Pastor's shoulder. "My house is yours. Oh, my, how long has it been?"

"Better part of a year."

"No! How can that be? Well, welcome to my home again."

Chango led Pastor into the former vice detective's spacious home and as they walked past a large wall mirror, Pastor saw his own reflection—graying, thinning hair, tired eyes, the image of a man, while far from being over the hill, was nonetheless clearly no longer young. He paused momentarily.

"I could use a vacation right about now."

"Can't we all?"

Chango took them into a waiting room furnished with a large sofa and several comfortable chairs. A tall, skinny man, tough looking, stood silently at one end of the couch, onto which Chango plopped familiarly. Pastor remained standing.

"Maria's not home?" He looked around the room, taking another quick look at the tall, skinny man.

"Unfortunately, no." Chango waved his arm. "She is with her family in Ixtapa. She will be so disappointed she missed you."

"Be sure to give her my love."

"Of course."

Chango took a large cigar out of case sitting on top of a long wooden table in front of the sofa. The skinny man hustled over to light it.

"Thank you, Chuy."

Pastor and Chuy again eyed each other closely.

"Cigar, Juanito?" Chango offered.

"No thanks."

"As yet no vices, *ey amigo*?"

Pastor surreptitiously fondled the pack of cigarettes he had inside his coat.

"You know me better than that, Chango."

"Yes—but, excuse my bad manners, would you care for a drink?"

"Yes, that would be good."

Chango signaled for Chuy to get the drinks. Pastor watched Chuy leave the room, as he did the maid briefly reappeared in the doorway, then hurried away

"I see you haven't lost your touch in choosing the household staff," Pastor chuckled.

"I... oh, I see. Still the old eye for the *Mexicanas*, yes?"

"I may be getting old, Chango, but I'm not dead yet."

Chango again laughed heartily. Chuy returned with the drinks, offering Pastor's first.

"*Muchas gracias*. I don't remember you, how long...."

"No, no, Juanito," Chango interrupted. "Chuy cannot speak. A little, how shall we say, accident when he was young and crossed Matanza."

"Matanza?" Pastor's eyes lit up.

"*Sí*, Matanza cut Chuy's tongue out. After that Chuy came to me. I gave him a job. He is loyal to me."

Chuy handed Chango his drink.

"*Gracias, joven.*"

Pastor studied Chuy, who resumed his position across the room.

"Matanza is the reason I came to see you, old friend."

"Yes?"

"Seems *Señor* Matanza and a gringo named Sonny Boston don't want me to solve a case I'm on. They sent a big goon to visit me. He's probably not walking too well today."

"Ah, yes, so you're the one they're looking for. This man said you robbed him and then shot him in the knee."

"I thought you'd retired from the police."

"I still have my... uh, contacts."

"No doubt. Maybe your contacts can get me a new place to live. The Hotel *El Parador* is a little hot right now."

"Don't worry, my friend." Chango said. "I'll call them off. I'll say you are a special Treasury agent. No problem."

"That would be good." Pastor said. "But I wasn't worrying too much anyway. I just want some leads, a lead."

"What was the case you were working on?"

"Missing girl."

"*Gringa*?"

"Yes. Her name is Anne Martin."

"Anne Martin?"

"You've heard of her?"

"No."

Pastor produced his wallet and showed Chango a photo of the girl.

"This is her?"

"Yes."

"Very nice."

"What do you think's going on, Chango? Who's this girl? Why would somebody want to clean me just for trying to solve a missing persons case?"

"I don't know, but if Matanza has become involved, you can be sure there's big money in it somewhere. And probably drugs."

"Yeah, I figured that, too. It seemed like such a simple case—but, hey, this guy they sent nearly got me. He caught me off guard."

"You must stay on your toes, now."

"I will, but it was a big surprise."

"Perhaps you should check again with your clients. Who are they?"

"That's a good question, Chango. I got the job through my agency in Houston, which is normal, but they were vague about it. Still, it all seemed so straightforward at the time I didn't think to ask. Besides, I needed the money."

"Hmmm. Maybe I can help. I will make certain—uh, inquiries."

"I would appreciate it. It looks like I'm in with the heavy hitters again."

Chango got up from the couch and stood by Pastor, placing his arm around the big PI's shoulders.

"I'll see what I can do. Now we can relax and enjoy ourselves a bit?"

"Sounds good." Pastor sighed.

Chango clapped his hands. In seconds, the maid reappeared.

"Maria, *otra whiskey para el señor*. And I want you to see to all of my friend's needs. *Me entiendes?*"

The maid hustled out for his drink.

"She understood all that? Even the English?"

"All of it."

"I don't know, Chango, I haven't been feeling that great lately."

Chango raised his hand as if to stop Pastor's train of thought. The maid reentered the room with the drinks but stood off to one side of the men.

"It has been a long time for you, my friend," Chango said. "You must learn to forget."

"I've learned to live without some things," Pastor allowed.

"That's not the same. No man should learn to live without a woman."

Chango signaled to the maid, who brought the drinks over. He leaned over and whispered something to her. She glanced at Pastor, then lowered her eyes.

"Chango, you can't—" Pastor began.

"You cannot stop living, Juanito," Chango said, "you must learn to feel again. It has been four years now. Karen was a fair and loving woman. She would want you to."

"I don't know," Pastor said. "I just don't feel much alive these days. Sometimes I feel empty, dead. Or like a ghost floating in the air. No one can see me, no one can touch me."

The maid reached out and put her hand softly on Pastor's arm. He looked into her gentle eyes, the pain in his obvious and strong.

"You must come back to life, my friend. It is all we have."

"Yes." Pastor forced a smile for the maid.

—

Ralph "Sonny" Boston, trim, fortyish, with dark hair and fair skin, sat in a large plush leather chair behind a huge, oak desk. Through the picture window behind him, downtown Phoenix, all metal and glass, shimmered in the bright sunlight. A younger Latino man stood to one side of Boston, waiting for the shady land developer to speak.

"Tell your boss," Boston finally said in cold, measured tones, "that I am extremely displeased with his lack of discipline. Tell him that if he can't control his impulses it will adversely affect our—*arrangement.* I don't want personal spite interfering with this."

"But, *Señor* Boston," the young man said in a heavy accent.

"Don't interrupt." Boston raised a fine, thin, and well-manicured hand.

"Yes, sir."

"I will be coming to Mexico shortly, as soon as I wrap up some loose ends here. Do you understand?"

"*Sí, señor.*"

Boston turned to face the messenger. The young man tensed, nearly to military attention.

"Have your people be ready to pick me up in Mexico City. My people will call ahead."

"*Bueno, señor.*"

"I want you to tell him personally that I want no screw ups on this. I want him to back off. Nothing final yet. Is that clear?"

"Yes."

"Tell him that to his face."

"As you wish."

"You are dismissed." Boston spun in his chair to face the office window.

Reflected in the window, the messenger made a sign with the index and little fingers of his right hand raised. Boston saw the gesture and a grim smile creased his white face.

When he spoke now, his voice was colder even than before.

"Get out. Now."

The messenger quickly turned and exited the office.

—

Pastor stood near the check-in counter in the main lobby of the upscale Hotel Sevilla talking on a house telephone. The clerk, a young energetic man, shuffled papers on the counter and pretended not to be listening to Pastor's side of the conversation.

"You found something on the girl, Chango? Most excellent. She was at the university and involved with the Museum of Anthropology, something happened and she disappeared. Got it."

Pastor noticed the clerk listening and turned away, presenting his back to the young man.

"It was in the papers here? Sounds like somebody else is maybe looking for her. What does that mean? I'm thinking someone in Houston thinks she's still alive. And the Matanza crowd doesn't seem to want me to find out one way or the other. You get any reading on that angle of it?"

Pastor glanced briefly at the clerk who continued to shuffle papers and act disinterested.

"Any leads at all? Professor Garcia from the university, now in Cuernavaca. The curator at the Cortes Palace down there. Great job, Chango. I knew I could count on you."

Pastor turned to hang up the phone but paused and spoke again.

"I will. I'm always careful. Trust me on that. See you, pal. And thanks again. I'll see you when I get back. *Ciao.*"

—

Pastor drove the winding road down to Cuernavaca, the Valley of Mexico and the thick smog of Mexico City falling away behind. Traffic was relatively light but it still took Pastor several minutes to realize that a dark compact car seemed to be following him.

As the highway declined in a sharp right turn signaling the descent into Cuernavaca, the volcano Popcatepetl looming on the hazy horizon, the car following Pastor suddenly pulled up alongside. The windows on the compact were shaded blocking Pastor's view of its interior but he could make out the shapes of two people within it. Hurtling downhill, side by side, the cars nearly sideswiped each other.

"What the hell?" Pastor exclaimed.

He tried slowing, then speeding up to escape the dark compact, but the vehicle stayed right beside him. Then, nearing another corner, the other vehicle intentionally pushed over into Pastor's lane and banged into the side of his car.

"Damn it."

Instinctively, Pastor jerked the car to the right but as he did, and seemingly from nowhere, a slow-moving horse-drawn cart appeared, trundling along the side of the road. In a flash, Pastor spotted an overgrown side road, more of a path than a real road and, barely missing the cart, he guided his car onto the path and came to a sliding, dusty halt. The dark compact shot by and disappeared around the next curve. Pastor leaned his head against the steering wheel and sighed.

"Sweet Jesus. What the hell was that?"

The horse-drawn cart rattled by, loud, popular Mexican music playing from a radio sitting on the seat by the cart driver. As the cart pulled alongside Pastor's temporarily stalled vehicle, the driver gave Pastor a friendly, toothless smile and a big wave. Pastor returned the smile and wave, then broke out laughing.

"I definitely need a vacation."

—

Professor Enrique Garcia, short, stocky, and white-haired, stood before a Diego Rivera mural on the second floor veranda of Cortes' Palace in downtown Cuernavaca. Two students jotted down notes as the professor animatedly described the colorful scene on the wall before them. Pastor approached from the landing on the second floor, but waited patiently until the students closed their notebooks and left the professor standing alone before the great mural.

"*Disculpamé. Profesor* Garcia?" Pastor stepped forward.

"Yes?" The professor turned toward Pastor, gave him a quick once-over then turned back to the mural.

"You speak English? You'd rather speak English?"

"Which question do you wish answered?"

"I'm sorry, professor." Pastor said. "I just…."

"Yes... and no. But you are North American. We speak English. How may I help you?"

"Thank you, sir. You're very courteous. My name is John Pastor. I'm here looking for a young woman."

"Aren't we all?"

Pastor started to speak, but the professor went on.

"Police?" He turned to size up Pastor more carefully. "From the U.S.?"

"No, sir, private detective. A friend of mine in Mexico City, a former policeman, said you might be able to help me."

"And who was this policeman?"

"Ephraim Morales."

"I don't know him."

"He's been off the police force several years."

"Smart man or perhaps he had taken enough *mordidas*—uh, bites—from the people, no?"

"I wouldn't know that, sir."

"No, of course you wouldn't."

"Would you like a drink, professor? I saw a pleasant cafe downstairs on the square."

"Yes, that would be nice."

Without speaking, they walked downstairs, out the broad doors of the castle and into the *jardín* proper. They only had to walk a few yards to find an outdoor cafe.

"Will this be all right?" Pastor pointed at a small, unoccupied, white wrought iron table with matching chairs sitting out from a small kiosk that served as the center of the tiny open air restaurant.

"Of course."

They sat down facing each other across the table and were shortly approached by a heavy set, smiling waiter.

"*Señores, algo para tomar?*"

"*Una copita de brandy*," the professor ordered. "*Lo mejor.*"

"*Si, señor. Y usted?*"

"Tequila and a glass of beer," Pastor said.

"Yes, sir," the waiter effortlessly switched to English. "Right away."

"Tell me, Mister, uh...." the professor began when the waiter had gone.

"Pastor."

"Mr. Pastor. Do you enjoy the murals of Diego Rivera?"

"Very much so."

"And have you seen the great ones in the Palace of Fine Arts and at the National Palace in Mexico City?"

"Yes, sir. Many times."

The waiter brought the drinks, creating another pause in the conversation. Pastor handed him *peso* bills.

"*Gracias, señor.* Would you like to order something to eat?"

"Not for me," Pastor said. "Professor?"

The professor waved off the offer with a wagged index finger. The waiter bowed and returned to his station near the kiosk.

"*Salud.*" The professor raised his glass.

"*Salud.*" Pastor echoed, lifting his beer as well.

"Now," the professor set his glass down on the table, "where were we, Mister Pastor?"

"I was telling you about my policeman friend. He said you might be able to help me find a former student of yours. A young North American woman."

"Anne Martin."

"Uh, yes, sir, that's the girl. You know her? Then she was your student?"

"Yes. A bright girl, quite lovely. She stayed with my family in Mexico City."

"You've just moved here to Cuernavaca?"

"Yes, I am retired now. We left to get away from the *contaminación*, the pollution. It is much cleaner here, but getting worse all the time. The weekends are terrible. We *Chilangos* are ruining this place, too. You know that term *Chilango*, for Mexico City people?"

"Yes, sir, I do. So when did you last see her then?"

"Who?" The professor turned and signaled to the waiter for another *copita*.

"Anne Martin." Pastor waved off the waiter for himself. He needed to refocus the professor, who seemed to be drifting a bit. "Anne Martin your student, remember?"

"Oh, yes. Well, I don't know," the professor said, "she left a few months ago now. No more than four or five. Before we moved."

"Do you know what happened to her, where she went?"

"*Piedra de Sangre.*"

"I'm sorry."

"Uh, how would you say… blood, bloodstone."

"Bloodstone. I don't understand."

"*Algo mas,*" the waiter arrived with the professor's drink. "Anything else."

"*No, gracias,*" the professor declined.

"What is this bloodstone?" Pastor asked when the waiter had gone.

"Bloodstone," the professor explained, "it is a name given to a special knife that legend says was used by the Aztecs to sacrifice humans. It is a stone knife, with the handles made of jade and a large ruby on the top side of one handle. It is priceless. It was stolen from the National Museum of Anthropology in the 1930s."

"Sounds like it would be worth a fortune," Pastor whistled.

"Indeed."

"The 1930s, you say? Now what would Anne Martin have to do with that, sir?"

"You must understand, *señor*, Ana was in love with all things Mexican. Its history, its culture, its ruins. Its men. When she read about the knife, the bloodstone, she could think of nothing else. It was an obsession for her. And it possessed her, changed her."

"How so?"

"She became friends with bad people; robbers, drug people. *Gringos* and *Mexicanos*. There were break-ins at the museum again. The police came to our house once. Then she was gone."

"Gone where?"

"*Quien sabe?* Who knows? Perhaps to Teotihuacan, perhaps Palenque. The rumors always trace the stone back to the great ruins."

"And do you believe the rumors, professor?"

"It was said that the men who stole the knife were patriots. That they wanted to return the knife to the ruins, to its rightful owners—the spirits of the mighty Aztecs."

"And you, what do you think?"

"I think they were thieves. Plain and simple. And that the stone has been sold, probably to a rich *gringo* or someone far away, perhaps in South America. It doesn't matter."

"It must have to Anne Martin." Pastor finished his drink and pushed the glass to the center of the table.

"She was foolish," the professor declared, "or became so."

"By the way, this is the same girl we're talking about, right?" Pastor held out a picture for the professor to see.

"Yes, it's her."

"One last thing." Pastor scratched his head and glanced around the public square.

"Yes?"

"You must have known Anne Martin quite well. Why didn't you report her missing?"

"I did. The police did nothing."

"You didn't follow it up?"

"What could I do? I am an old man."

"Maybe she just went home."

"Perhaps."

"If you were in my place, professor, where would you try next?"

Professor Garcia extracted a thin, elegant cigar from his coat pocket, lit it and blew a puff of smoke into the air. Pastor checked to see if he still had his pack of cigarettes. They were in his pocket, unopened.

"Teotihuacan," the professor said between puffs on his cigar, "the Temple of Quetzalcoatl. That is where I would begin."

"And what would I be looking for there?" Pastor wondered.

"Besides some rumor of the stone or the girl, I don't know, Mr. Pastor. You're the detective, no?"

"Yes, sir, I am." Pastor stood up.

"Mr. Pastor." The professor raised his hand to delay Pastor's departure.

"Yes?"

"If you go to Teotihuacan, and cleanse yourself of modern attitudes," the professor waxed near poetic, "then you may feel the spirits of the long dead floating on the wind. Their history will be alive for you and they may help you find the girl."

"Help me find the girl?" Pastor raised an eyebrow.

"For those without prejudice," the professor continued, "the past speaks to us of the present and the future, as well as the past."

"Uh, yeah, right. Thanks."

"*A sus ordenes*," the professor said.

"Well, sir," Pastor said, "thank you for your time."

"*Por nada.*"

"Whew, Pastor said to himself as he walked away. "Definitely *por nada*."

—

Pastor stood at the top of the steps leading from the main entrance of Teotihuacan to the Avenue of the Dead, a wide, grassy, pathway running the length of the great ruins. In the distance to his left, at the far end of the Avenue of the Dead, was the Pyramid of the Moon. Three-fourths of the way to it and on the right side of the pathway, the massive Pyramid of the Sun. Directly across from him, up a steep set of stone steps and then down on the other side, was the set of buildings known as the *Ciudadela*. At the back of this series of buildings was a large ancient temple and within it an even older one, the Temple of Quetzalcoatl, the legendary god of the ancient ones.

"What am I looking for here?" Pastor grumbled. He checked a small map he had of the ruins, folded it up, and then put it in his back pocket. "That damn Professor Garcia was nuttier than a fruitcake. This is just a tourist trap. Nothing will happen here."

With a resigned sigh, he walked on toward the *Ciudadela*. Focused on the flat field in front of him, Pastor went toward the Temple of Quetzalcoatl at the back of the *Ciudadela*, oblivious to the army of souvenir vendors milling around nearby.

"*Buenas tardes, señor.*" A male voice suddenly broke Pastor's concentration.

"What?" Pastor paused.

"Great are they not, the ruins?" the man attached to the voice said. He carried several trinkets commonly sold at the site.

"Oh, yes. Beautiful."

"Yes, beautiful. You maybe need a guide? I know this ruins well. I live here all my life. Close by. Here at the village." The man pointed to a scattered cluster of poor homes just beyond the back edge of the ruins.

"No," Pastor vacillated, "I, uh . . . well, okay. Yeah, how much?"

"You decide, *señor*, when we are done."

"Fair enough."

The guide led Pastor toward the entrance at the right side of the temple. They were briefly accompanied by a handful of little boys selling trinkets but by the time they reached the wooden walkway that passed through the open air interior of the old temple, only one little boy remained.

"The figures with the round eyes are Tlaloc, the god of rain," the guide explained. "The snake heads are Quetzalcoatl, the feathered serpent."

"*La serpienta enplumada,*" Pastor said.

"*Exactamente, señor.*" The guide seemed impressed.

Pastor noticed that a small crowd was forming around him and the guide, including the little trinket seller and an attractive woman in a white dress highlighted with small, dark polka dots.

"You can see this temple is inside the much newer one," the guide continued to his expanded audience.

"Yes." Pastor leaned forward to get a closer look at a Quetzalcoatl head.

"*Señor*, you are looking for something?"

"I don't know," Pastor straightened up, "this was Aztec? Where they performed their sacrifices?"

"No, sir," the guide said, "I think you are thinking of the Templo Mayor, in the *zocalo* in Mexico City. This place is older, much before the Aztecs."

"I see. And there would be nothing found here about the *piedra de sangre.*"

I don't know, *señor*, I...."

"Did you say *piedra de sangre?*" the lady in white interjected.

Pastor looked her over for the first time. She and her dress seemed out of place there in the archaeological zone.

"I'm sorry?" he said.

"Excuse me for butting in," the woman said, "but you are interested in the bloodstone?"

"Why yes, you've heard of it?"

"Everyone in Mexico knows of the *piedra de sangre*, sir. May I ask why you ask for it? It has been lost for nearly sixty years?"

"Yes, I know, I…."

"Hey, mister," the little vendor boy suddenly cried out, looking back at the top of the newer temple behind them. "*Mira*, look out! *Aguas*!"

Before Pastor or the others could react to the boy's warning, a bullet slapped off the temple stone in front of the group, splattering rock chips into the air. The report of a pistol sounded almost simultaneously and was quickly followed by another, then another round. Pastor leaped over and pushed the woman down against the wall behind them, protecting her with his body. The guide and the boy dove below the walkway for cover.

After a short pause in which no more shots were fired, Pastor leaned out to look up at the pyramid stretching above them and saw, for just an instant, the disappearing figure of the assailant. Pastor jumped up and raced along the walkway and out into the open field on the other side of the temple. A large curious crowd had formed and it was impossible to see where the assailant went. After a fruitless visual search, Pastor returned to the temple to find only the little boy and the guide.

"What happened to the woman?"

"She is gone, *señor*?"

"She went the other way, mister," the little vendor boy said.

"She was okay?"

"She was okay, I think."

"Thanks, pal," Pastor told the boy, patting the kid on the shoulder. "You did good."

Pastor looked over the boy's head toward the older temple wall across the wooden walkway and saw what looked like bullet holes from the attack. He walked over and began digging at the holes. At first he did not notice a new commotion to his left, but he looked up just in time to see several Mexican police enter from both sides of the walkway. Suddenly, he was surrounded by the police, their weapons drawn. Two of the policemen grabbed him.

"Hey, what? What the hell are you doing?"

Without a word, the officers drug Pastor away. The guide and little boy ran alongside.

"*Dejelo*," the little boy cried out, "*dejelo, cabrones*. Let him go, you bastards. Let him go."

One of the officers stopped and turned menacingly toward the guide and boy. They stopped following immediately. The police hauled Pastor away without further incident.

—

"Let's try this again, Mister Pastor," the representative of the U. S. Consulate in Mexico City said, "if you please. Why would anyone want to shoot at you?"

Pastor sat in a plush office chair and stared at the low-level bureaucrat's nameplate sitting atop the solid, heavy wood desk—Austin Rogers, M. A.

Rogers thumbed through a dossier he had open before him. Pastor felt more inclined to avert his eyes to the window and take in the lush vegetation on the consulate grounds than listen to the shrewish embassy man.

"Mister Pastor, did you hear me?"

"Gee, Mister—uh, Rogers, I wouldn't know. I was too busy defacing the temple when I was arrested to notice any shooting, you know."

"Not funny, Pastor." Rogers stood up. "You know you're lucky to be out of jail in the first place. I can't imagine how you managed it."

"I'm well liked locally."

"It says here in your file," Rogers grunted, looking over the dossier while he walked back and forth behind his desk, "that you're some sort of private detective, whatever that might mean down here."

"By the way, where's Collins anyway? He used to be—"

"My, my," Rogers answered, "we are out of touch, aren't we? Mr. Collins rotated several months ago."

"Swell."

"Born, Rochester, Minnesota," Rogers read from the dossier. "Divorced. Army, Gulf Wars era. But no actual war zone experience. You missed the major conflicts of your generation?"

"Not everybody could go. Just my good luck."

"And then the border patrol in New Mexico. Officer terminated for unspecified reasons. Interesting. Would you care to elaborate, Mister Pastor?"

"It's personal."

"On a need to know basis, I suppose?"

"Something like that."

"I don't know who you know, Pastor," Rogers tossed the dossier down with some force, "that is willing to save your neck and dump you on us, but you're our responsibility now and you'd best go along with the program if you want to keep that license of yours."

"Listen," Pastor countered, "I've told you everything I know. I don't have any idea what went on out there. It's as big a mystery to me as it is to you or anyone else. Now, if you don't mind, I'd like to get back to work."

"Negative, Mister Pastor, you're not going anywhere. The Mexican government has forbidden you to visit Teotihuacan again."

"What?"

"That's right, mister, the ruins are off limits to you."

"You gotta be kidding me." Pastor did not smile. "Get serious."

"Oh, it's serious all right," Rogers assured him. "So serious, in fact, that if I were you, I'd consider leaving Mexico."

"Leave?" Pastor stood, facing the bureaucrat. "Is that some kind of deportation threat, Rogers? I'm not amused."

"We never *threaten*, Mister Pastor." Rogers backed up a step behind the desk. "You're free to stay in Mexico—at present—but if you do choose to remain, stay away from the archaeological zones. The government would like for them to last a while longer."

"You're a real funny guy, Rogers. A real bright boy."

"Good day, Mister Pastor. I have other, more urgent, business."

"Have a nice day, Mr. Rogers." Pastor leaned over the table. Rogers stiffened, but didn't move. After a moment, Pastor straightened up with a laugh. "What a load of crap." He turned and headed for the door.

"You will," Rogers said to Pastor's back, "keep us informed about your activities, Mister Pastor? That is, if you're planning on getting shot at again."

"*Chinga su madre*," Pastor snorted as he stepped into the hallway.

"I understood," Rogers fumed, "I understood that perfectly well."

"Good, I hate to waste a nice descriptive phrase like that." Pastor shut the door solidly behind him, leaving Rogers alone to stew in his ambassadorial juices.

—

José Matanza lived in decadent luxury. His palatial estate in the Coyoacan section of Mexico City was the finest illegal money could buy. His living room was bigger than most houses in Mexico and a large family could have easily lived there. He had bodyguards in practically every room, as befitted a man of his stature, and provocatively dressed young women attended to his every need. He drank expensive whiskey from large, fine crystal glasses and had three chefs who catered to his every comestible whim. The one thing missing from this magnificent home was Mrs. Matanza. Long ago she had made a separate peace with José and had been rewarded with a home in Cuernavaca where she lived in luxury herself. It was a nice arrangement and Matanza prided himself on his generosity.

"Bring me some snow," he told one of the barely dressed girls, "I need to cool down before I get too hot."

The girl giggled becomingly and Matanza gave her a swat on the derriere as she hustled off. A phone buzzed across the room and Matanza cocked an ear toward the sound. The call was to one of his bodyguards.

"*Bueno*," the bodyguard, a tall, heavy-muscled man, answered. "*Si.* Okay."

"*Quien fue?*" Matanza said. "Who was it?"

"Pedro," the tall bodyguard answered. "They are arriving from the airport soon."

"*Muy bien*. Go meet them."

"*Si, jefe.*" The bodyguard walked briskly to the door. He had just gone when the young woman came back into the room. She carried a mirror with several lines of white powder on it.

"*Un espejo de nieve*," Matanza said, "a mirror of snow."

"*Loco*," the girl said.

"Come, my lovely." Matanza pulled the girl to him and reached inside her loose fitting top. "*Dame la cocaina*. Give me the cocaine."

"Here, José," she said, "take it."

"Food of the gods." Matanza let go of the girl, bent to the mirror and deftly snorted the two white lines.

He handed the mirror back to the girl. She licked a finely manicured finger, ran it over the mirror and tasted what was left of the cocaine. Matanza took a big swig of whiskey. He patted the girl on the bottom and kissed her. The front door bell rang and Matanza released the girl.

"*Momentito*," he called over his shoulder.

She rose and began to move away. Matanza gave her another swat on the rear and stood up on the couch. Another bodyguard, this one short and heavy-set, appeared from the interior of the house. Matanza signaled him to stand to one side the door.

"*Adelante*," Matanza said loudly. "Come in."

The door opened, the tall bodyguard held it for a thin, well dressed man who entered the home like it was his own.

"Sonny!" Matanza extended his hand, "welcome to my poor home."

Sonny Boston walked right past the proffered handshake, stopped a few feet past Matanza and did a loose about face.

"I thought you could handle this, Matanza."

"Thank you for coming." Matanza bowed extravagantly.

"No beating around the bush, José." Boston ignored the gesture. "You need to take care of this."

"Anything to eat or drink, perhaps some company."

"Don't be ridiculous," Boston said. "There's no time for social amenities. We, you have a problem. You need to take care of it."

"I'm handling it," Matanza assured his visitor.

"It doesn't sound like it to me. The *Federales* and the U.S. government involved, that's what you call handling it?"

"It's under control. No problem."

"It's going to be a problem, José, if you don't start curbing your excesses."

"Sure you don't want anything to drink, Sonny?" Matanza ignored Boston's scolding.

"Forget the damn drinks. I don't like the way this is going down."

"You worry too much, my friend. You should learn to relax. Perhaps a woman would help."

"No."

"You must have had at some time—to have a daughter."

"*Step*daughter."

"Oh, I see."

"You see nothing, José, and I don't need any of your south of the border psychology."

"Very well." Matanza's eyes flared briefly but he managed a forced smile.

"There's a job to do down here," Boston told him. "I suggest you, we, get it done and done right."

"Sonny, Sonny, we've worked together before. It has been profitable, no? The plan is working."

"Working?" Boston grunted. "What about this guy, this—detective that my loving ex hired to find Anne?"

"I know him. From years ago." Matanza said. "His name is Pastor. He's a fool."

"Well, that fool is getting in our way."

"He will soon no longer be a hindrance to us."

"José, that attitude is exactly why we have a problem. We agreed to discourage Pastor while your people were looking for Anne, not kill him. Your men came too close. We don't need the *Federales* linking us to a murder. We just want the guy to back off."

"He is a *gringo, gordo y estupido*, fat and stupid. The rest was done as you ordered. I still think we should get him out of the way."

"I don't know what you have against this guy personally, but restrain your impulse to kill him. There's too much at stake here, José. We have too much to lose. Keep Pastor away, in the dark, but keep him alive. A murder investigation could bring us down."

"Don't worry, it's all taken care of."

"Okay. So, how close are your people to finding Anne?"

"We have been distracted by the *gringo* detective." Matanza avoided direct eye contact with Boston. "But we are nearing her."

"I've heard enough about the detective, if he gets too close, scare him off again. But where is Anne? Where is my daughter?"

"*Step*daughter," Matanza smiled again, couldn't resist the dig. Boston rolled his eyes. "Our sources say she and her 'companions' are in hiding somewhere to the east."

"That's all you have?" Boston said. "Somewhere to the east. Where to the east, Japan?"

"There is a rumor about the Equinox in the Yucatan."

"A rumor about the Equinox in the Yucatan? That's what you've got to tell me? What the hell does that mean?"

"It means we're getting close and that my men are working on it."

"Jesus, José, this damn hack detective will probably find her before you do. Maybe we should just follow him and then take over when he finds Anne."

"Impossible. He is too slow. This is my country. I know it. Everything is under control."

"You keep saying that."

"We're on top of it, I tell you."

"Well, see that it stays that way."

"No problem." Matanza jutted out his jaw. "We got it covered."

—

Chapultepec Park was typically busy with joggers, families and couples enjoying a day out and, of course, many foreign tourists drawn to this green oasis in the heart of Mexico City itself. Pastor and Chango Morales strolled casually among the throng, two of the ex-detective's men following unobtrusively several yards behind. The path they followed led slowly upward, winding around toward the great castle atop a high hill overlooking the park and city.

"I don't like it, Chango." Pastor said as quietly as he could and still be heard above the ambient sound in the park. "There's something really fishy about all this. A lot of the pieces don't fit together. I went to see the professor and nearly got driven off the mountain on the way to Cuernavaca. He knew the girl and suggested I go to Teotihuacan. So I go there and all of a sudden somebody, I have to assume another one of Boston and Matanza's "messengers," takes a shot me… but not trying to hit me, just scare me off. And then there was this woman."

"A woman?"

"Yes. She was there and then disappeared right after the shots. Before the police got there."

"And you think she's part of it, too, Juanito?"

"No, definitely not part of the shooting. But, I don't know, I'm sure she wasn't just a *turista*. She had that Mexico City look."

"*Chilanga*?"

"I think so."

As they neared the top of the hill and the great castle where Moctezuma II occupied the last Aztec throne, Chango stopped at a small vendor cart for a cup of ice cream.

"Juanito? Would you like some?"

"No, no thanks, Chango."

"Suit yourself."

"The plain truth is," Pastor continued as they walked on, Chango savoring the ice cream, "I'm not sure where to go next. Some people, Sonny Boston, our old buddy Matanza, the police, maybe even my own government, don't seem to want me to find this girl. What the hell's up?"

"Maybe you should drop the case?"

"No can do." Pastor raised an eyebrow at Chango's suggestion. "I called the Houston office, they've upped the ante."

"And did you find out who it is that's paying you?"

"No. You know, it's funny, it's like one side wants me to back off and the other one wants me to go for it. Something is going on here but I don't get what it is yet. Maybe I'm too old for this kind of work anymore."

"You are just tired, my friend, in the *alma*, the soul."

"Perhaps."

"You will be better soon, Juanito, I know you. You won't quit. You will get better. Perhaps this job is what you need to live again."

"I'd rather take a vacation in the Yucatan."

"Not a bad idea, the Yucatan is always a good place to relax. But, today, *amigo*, how can I help you?"

"Where should I look next? I wasn't finding anything out at Teo when whoever it was decided I had a bullseye on my butt. All I know is this girl loves Mexicans and Mexican artifacts and Mexican ruins. Shit, Chango, you know how many ruins there are in this country. More ruins than—"

"Monte Alban."

"Monte Alban?"

"Monte Alban."

"Why there, Chango? Why not Tulum, Chichen Itza, Palenque… Monte Alban is down south, by Oaxaca. It's sort of off the main trail."

"Exactly. A quiet place, maybe, for the girl and her people to disappear into. With so many people interested in your activities… well, you see? Perhaps there, a few questions in the proper places."

"And, bingo, I find the girl, right?"

"Why not?" Chango answered as they reached historic Chapultepec Castle. "Ah, the great Castle of Moctezuma. The last stronghold of our indigenous peoples against the Spaniards."

"And where the young heroes of the Mexican-American War leaped to their death rather than surrender to the U.S. Army," Pastor added.

"We have always been invaded," Chango lamented. "Outsiders always getting their noses into our business."

"True enough, Chango." Pastor sighed. "If I'm going to find the girl, I've gotta stick my nose into it some more, too."

"Just be careful. That which sticks out is that which is cut off first."

"Thanks, old buddy. A real pleasant thought."

"Be careful, but keep looking. You will find what you need to."

"Down in Oaxaca, huh? That's a heck of a long way away. I guess I better get rolling. They're not paying me to visit the park, huh?"

"I suppose not," Chango said.

"See you, Chango. Thanks."

"*Vaya con Dios, mi amigo*, may God go with you."

"Uh-huh." Pastor walked away, on down the hill.

"Keep in touch, Johnny," Chango called after him. "I mean it."

"I'll send you a post card from Monte Alban."

"*Nos vemos*."

Pastor waved his right arm without looking back.

—

The Mexicana Airlines 727 touched down at Oaxaca's Xoxocotlán Airport around mid-day. Disembarking, Pastor crossed the tarmac, feeling the warmth and humidity of the lushly green Oaxaca Valley and entered the small, but modern, terminal. Inside, he quickly spotted the ever-present *taxistas* and was whisked outside to a waiting van. Climbing in with several other people, he settled in for the ride into town.

He chose a nice hotel downtown, just off the *jardín*, called the Del Valle. After putting his things up and refreshing a bit, he decided to reconnoiter the town center and get the lay of the land. The plaza, small by Mexican standards, was nonetheless typical for the country. It was a square with a clean, tree-filled park at its center and open air restaurants filled with tourists, primarily Europeans, enjoying food and drinks around its sides.

The feature making Oaxaca's plaza different from most others in the country was the placement of the main cathedral. Instead of being in or on the plaza itself, the cathedral was to one side—just off the plaza.

After checking the plaza sights out, Pastor began a systematic check. He went in and out of travel agencies, stores, and cafes showing the picture of Anne Martin to anyone who would look at it. He received many strange looks but nothing overtly hostile or suspicious. At least he couldn't see anyone following him and no one seemed concerned enough to take a shot at him like at Teotihuacan. Finally, he was in front of the local tourist office. He paused, considered the outside of the building for several minutes, then pushed open the door.

Inside the leaflet and poster filled tourist office, Pastor discovered it was empty. He walked around for a moment reading the many signs expounding the cultural highlights of the city and region. Finding an interesting brochure, he skimmed that until he heard someone clear their throat behind me.

"May I help you, sir?" Pastor turned to see an office girl smiling at him.

"Well, hello, *señorita. Buenos dias*."

"*Buenos dias, señor.* Can I do anything for you?"

"Hmm." Pastor considered the possibilities.

He reached into his pocket for the picture of Anne Martin but paused, re-pocketed it and instead pointed to a picture of Monte Alban on the wall.

"Yes, you can help me. Can you tell me how to get up there, to the ruins? I want to go to Monte Alban."

"The bus leaves from behind the Presidente Juarez, sir," the girl explained. "It is at the corner of Toltec and Uruguay. Only three blocks away from here, on the same street as the *mercado*. You know the marketplace?"

"I can find it, thanks. Oh—uh, how often does it go?"

"At least every hour, sir. On busy days, every thirty minutes."

"Can I get a guide here?"

"No, sir, but there are always guides at Monte Alban."

"You don't do that?"

"No, sir."

"Well, it was worth a shot," Pastor said softly.

"I'm sorry, sir?"

"Never mind, miss. Thank you."

"*Gracias a usted, señor.*"

Pastor waved his left hand in goodbye and stepped through the door back into the street.

—

Pastor climbed up into the bus and handed his ticket to the driver who tore it in two and handed half back. He went down the aisle, past a combination of local and foreign tourists, fewer than he expected, until he found an empty seat in which to plop down. Bored, he drummed his fingers on the back of the seat in front of him until its occupants, a young European couple turned around.

"Oh… sorry." He looked at his hands as if they had done something over which he had no control. When the couple turned back around Pastor flipped them off.

After another quarter hour, the driver finally shut the door and the worn-out vehicle lurched forward. Just as the bus exited the hotel parking lot, Pastor caught movement in his peripheral vision. He quickly turned and for the briefest moment thought he saw a woman dressed in white peasant clothes standing at the back door of the hotel. He whipped around to see but the door was empty. No sign of the woman. He watched the hotel until the bus rounded a corner and the hotel disappeared from sight.

"No way," he scratched his head. "Couldn't be. Could not be."

—

Beneath a bright sun and clear blue sky, from the ruins high atop the mountain, Pastor had a 360 degree view of the valleys stretching out below and beyond Monte Alban. A light wind blew, providing some relief from the intensity of the pre-tropical heat.

While he absorbed the remarkable beauty of the vista in relative peace away from the handful of other tourists on the day excursion, a few vendors, dressed like "town" *campesinos* in dark cotton pants, long sleeved, faded plaid shirts, sandals with no socks, and straw hats, slowly emerged among the ruins. They appeared benign enough, but their appearance coupled with his recent experience at other Mexican ruins gave him pause.

"*Hola, señor,*" one of them addressed Pastor, "do you want to buy a stone from the pyramids? Been here hundreds years. See, mister, right here I have it. It was in the ground for many, many years. I found it myself."

Pastor examined the proffered "artifact," noting immediately its obvious mass-produced quality.

"No, thank you."

"But it is," the vendor insisted, "uh, hen-oo-ine."

"Of course, genuine. I am sure, friend. But no. *Gracias*, no."

The vendor began to move away, but Pastor called him back.

"Wait, *amigo*, hold up." When the man turned back, Pastor showed him the map of the ruins he had picked up back in Oaxaca. "Where can I find this tomb, Tomb 118?"

"Over there, *señor.*" The vendor pointed, after looking over the map. "On the other side of this field. There are several. Tomb 118 is there. Over there."

"*Muchas gracias.*"

"*Por nada.*"

Pastor followed the directions and walked along a dirt path looking for the tomb that once gave up a fortune in burial treasure but was now kept up and protected by the state. Stopping briefly, he looked around and spotted an area below the rise on which he stood, a small opening to one of the tombs.

He clambered down the rise, dust puffing up behind his shoes, to the tomb. In the process, he nearly crashed into another man he had not seen who stood beside some bushes near the tomb.

"Whoa, excuse me. *Dispenseme.*"

The man silently stared back at Pastor.

"Can you tell me, is this Tomb 118, uh, es esta la tumba cien zero...."

"*Sí señor,*" the man finally said, "this is 118."

"Great, this is supposed to be a good one."

"Yes, good."

The man walked beside Pastor the last few feet to the tomb.

"You climb down in here to see it?" Pastor eyed the man warily.

"Climb down," the man said. Pastor hesitated. "No, you must climb down. It's in there."

Pastor started down the steps, then paused.

"You go first."

"No, no," the man declined. "*Pase, pase usted.* Go ahead."

"All right."

Pastor continued down the stairs, shoulders hunched as if he expected to receive a blow at any moment. When the blow was not forthcoming, he relaxed and climbed on down into the narrow tomb.

At the bottom of the stairs, behind bars, was the well-preserved tomb, final resting place perhaps of some great but nameless Zapotec aristocrat. The walls were painted in geometric designs and with representations of animals and birds. Pastor peered forward to get a better look, then turned back.

Suddenly the man leapt down into the tomb and struck Pastor's head with a fist-sized rock. Blood spurted from above Pastor's temple and he crashed down in the tomb, slamming against the iron bars.

The man, flailing away, landed on top.

"You son of a bitch." Pastor struggled to dodge repeated blows with the rock.

In the melee, they wrestled around, exchanging relatively ineffective punches, until Pastor managed to free his right hand and delivered one, then another, sharp right crosses to the man's face. The man slumped down against the bars that protected the murals and artifacts in the tomb.

Panting, sweating, and bleeding, Pastor stood above the man for a moment recomposing himself. Impulsively, he searched the man. In a front shirt pocket, he was surprised to find a bad snapshot of himself. He turned it over to see one word written on the back: *Palenque.*

"*Palenque?*" He deposited the photo in his own pocket and began to climb up out of the tomb. "*Palenque*, for God's sakes, where the hell next?"

Just as he was nearing the opening of the tomb, without warning the man leaped up from below and grabbed Pastor's legs and feet. Hanging onto the stairs, he again struggled with the man, then extracted his right leg and dealt him a crushing kick to the head. The man plummeted backward with a cry, the back of his head slamming into a slab of rock on the floor of the tomb. Blood trickled out from behind his head.

"Rest in peace, *pendejo.*"

Pastor hustled up and out of the tomb.

—

Pastor, a bandage on the side of his head from the battle of the previous day, ordered a light breakfast of fruit and cereal at an open-air cafe on the plaza in Oaxaca. As he ate, he read from the English-language daily, The *Mexico City Times*. Absorbed in the paper, he did not notice two men in dark suits until they stood next to his table.

"Good morning, *señor,*" one of the men greeted him.

Pastor looked up from his paper and immediately recognized policemen, even in plainclothes, even in a foreign country.

"I might have known."

The first cop raised an eyebrow. "Sir?"

"Never mind. I don't suppose you're here to deal with my complaint about the service?"

"You will please come with us, Mister Pastor."

"Oh, you know my name, uh? How did you—"

"We just want to ask you some questions."

"Isn't this where I ask you for ID, for your badges?" Pastor rose, tossing his newspaper and some Mexican coins on the table. Nearby breakfasters tried to act as if they weren't watching what was going on.

"Badges?" The second cop exchanged looks with his partner.

"Forget it." Pastor said.

The police, one on either side, walked him away. Breakfast went on at the cafe as if nothing had happened.

—

In less than a quarter of an hour, Pastor found himself at police headquarters in a dingy room lit only by one grimy window and a weak 60-watt bulb.

"Tell me again," a gruff sergeant grilled him, while the two plainclothesmen stood to one side, "how did you hurt your head?"

"I ran into the side of my hotel room door."

"This is not a joke, mister," the sergeant said. "A man was found nearly dead on Monte Alban. We have people who say you were there, too."

Pastor was silent.

"*Mira, amigo,*" the sergeant stepped up close to Pastor, "we know you were at Monte Alban. Other people say they saw you going to where the man was attacked. Just before it happened."

"Do I get to call a lawyer? I want to call the U.S. Consulate."

"Why are you here in Oaxaca, *Señor* Pastor?" The sergeant took a step back.

"I heard people here were real friendly."

"This is a serious matter," the first plainclothesman said. "Please, you must cooperate."

"I'm sorry, officer. I know nothing of this attack. I only arrived in Oaxaca yesterday. I haven't been to Monte Alban."

"Perhaps if you and I went over this alone," the sergeant suggested, "your memory would improve."

"*Disculpame, sargento.*" A police clerk entered the room. "*Hay un mensaje.* There's a message for you." He and the sergeant conferred quietly for a moment, then the clerk hustled back out of the room.

"Come with us, *inmediatamente,*" the sergeant ordered. "Right now."

"Where are we going? What for?"

"Come along." The first plainclothesman took Pastor's arm.

The officers led, occasionally tugged, Pastor down a corridor into the main lobby of the police station. It was busy with policemen and a passel of ragged looking suspects. At the central desk another clerk handed over what few of Pastor's belongings the police had confiscated.

"Here are your things." The sergeant pushed them toward Pastor.

"What's going on?"

"You're free to go," the first plainclothesman said.

'What? Why? I mean—"

"You have been cleared by the authorities," the sergeant explained. "You may go."

"Great. What authorities are you talking about? What does that make you guys? Who sprang me?"

The first plainclothesman nodded to their left. Pastor followed the officer's motion.

"You." He saw the Mexican woman who had been at Teotihuacan—and lord only knew where else that she had been, too. "Well, I'll be a son of a gun. It *was* you back at the hotel."

"I am Claudia Santiago." She crossed the room to shake hands. "I'm happy to meet you."

"Likewise I'm sure." He took her hand in his as if it might be something venomous. "You're getting me out of this place?"

"Yes."

"Swell, and thanks. You mind explaining why and what's going on?"

"Soon. After we leave. Are you hungry, Mister Pastor?"

"It's John, call me John. And yes I am. I didn't quite finish my breakfast this morning." He looked over at the sergeant and two plainclothesmen.

The sergeant glared back, but the first plainclothesman smiled.

"It was fun, fellows," Pastor called back over his shoulder as he and Claudia headed out the police station door. "We should do this more often. Room service was great."

—

Pastor and Claudia found another of Oaxaca's open-air cafes where he filled up on *queso fundido* and corn tortillas and she sipped on a dark liqueur, begging off from midafternoon food. Leaning back in his chair after the meal, Pastor savored a cold Superior and sized Claudia up. She was probably in her late thirties and judging from her fashionable clothes and sparkling eyes, well off and intelligent.

"What is it, John?"

"You've been following me ever since Teotihuacan. Hell, maybe before that. Why?"

"You're welcome."

"I said thanks at the station."

"Yes, I know you did."

"So, what's the deal here?"

"Can't we just enjoy our drinks a moment, and absorb this beautiful place. Look at all the interesting people here in the little plaza. This is Mexico, John, it should be enjoyed."

"Listen, lady, in the last ten days I've looked down the barrel of a hit man's gun, been run off the road, shot at in Teotihuacan and rousted out by the U.S. Consulate. I've been beaten up down here and hauled in by your local gendarmes. Most of it because I followed the advice of someone I think, thought, is a friend back in Mexico City and, funny thing, on top of it all, you seem to pop up at all these odd times along the way, too."

"John—"

"Just a minute, and for your information, Miss Claudia Whoever the Hell You Are, I love this country and its people, too. I've lived here a while now. I'm no longer a *turista*. And this is *not* my idea of enjoying beautiful Mexico. I don't know what your game is and I don't know who thinks it's great fun watching the *gringo* go through his paces, but I've just about had it with this crap. Right now, you can take the ruins and whatever games you people are playing and... and... hell, I don't know what you can do with them, but you can count me out."

With a flourish at the end of his impassioned speech, Pastor pulled out the pack of cigarettes he'd been carrying since Mexico City and the *El Parador* and started to open them.

"I haven't seen you smoke before." Claudia put her hand out to stop him. "I didn't know you did."

"You don't know anything about me."

"I know that you don't need these."

"Oh, yeah?"

"I don't want to see you harm yourself just because you're upset, John."

"I'm not upset."

"Then do it to please me."

"That's what she used to say." Pastor slowly lowered the cigarette pack and re-pocketed it. "Sorry about that. A momentary lapse. I've been having a bit of a rough time lately. Forgive me?"

"No need, but already done."

Claudia reached in a small handbag and pulled out the snapshot of Pastor he had taken from his attacker up at Monte Alban. She slid it across the table. He picked it up and turned it over to again see the word "*Palenque*" written on the back. He looked over at Claudia. She gave him a sultry smile, full of seductive promise.

"Boy, you got it all, don't you?" he said.

"I can help you find the girl you're after."

"Who said I was after a girl?"

"We think she may be living with a drug cult in the jungle near Palenque. This photo certainly seems to back that up. How did you come by it?"

"We? Who's we?"

"In the '60s, your hippies and our hippies moved out there and lived together in a… uh…."

"Commune?"

"Yes, commune. Mushrooms grow there, many. And it is a good place for drug smugglers to hide."

"Why do you care about this girl that I'm supposed to be trying to find? What's she to you? Whoever you or we are."

"John, the girl only matters because she and whoever she is with have or know where to find a stolen national treasure. A valuable one."

Pastor took a drink of beer and acted like he had no idea what Claudia was talking about.

"We could work together. You get the girl, we get our national treasure back."

Pastor looked away, out across the plaza to the many couples and vendors filling the park.

"Please, John, come with me, come with me to Palenque."

Pastor sized her up from head to foot, looked into her brown eyes as if he could read into her soul—or at least into her motives.

"What the heck, woman." He leaned back in his chair with a laugh. "Why not. I love vacationing in these ruins. They're my life. I can't get enough of them."

—

The late night streets of Villahermosa were freshly rain wet and deserted as the taxi rolled through the city, only occasionally passing another vehicle. Claudia slept in the back seat, resting against Pastor's shoulder. Awake, he eyed her warily, occasionally attempting to move slightly away.

As the taxi passed through an intersection, a large, older model Chevrolet came out of a side road and pulled up closely behind the smaller vehicle, a newer, but considerably used, Toyota. The driver checked the rear view mirror and sped up a little. The Chevrolet stayed on his bumper, its lights sporadically illuminating the taxi interior.

"What's going on?" Pastor looked back at the pursuing vehicle.

"*Yo no se, señor.* I don't know," the *taxista* said. "All of a sudden the car, it was just there."

"How far to the hotel?"

"Just a few blocks, *señor.*"

"Step on it. Lose these *cabrones.*"

"*Sí, señor.*"

"What's happening?" Claudia woke as the taxi sped up and swerved around a corner. The cars sped down a wide avenue.

"Looks like we got somebody on our tail."

"*Ay, cuidado, putos,*" the driver cried out as the trailing vehicle's occupants opened fire on the taxi with handguns. "*Chinga su madre,*" he yelped when his outside mirror was suddenly blasted away.

Jerking the car to the right, the driver spun down a side street in front of a late-running truck. The pursuers barely made the side street turn but unleashed another barrage of fire, bullets whistling by the taxi to splat against the walls of fronting buildings. With an adroit maneuver, the driver slid the taxi into a dark, narrow alley. As they rushed down it, the alley got more and more narrow as it neared its upcoming exit.

"Oh, shit." Pastor grabbed Claudia and held her tight. "Hang on."

As he did, the taxi, sides scraping the alley walls, exploded out the other side onto a regular-sized road. Behind them the Chevy, sparks flying, ripped along building fronts and then came to a sudden, metal-tearing halt against the sides of the alley. Pastor saw its occupants slammed against windows, doors, and windshield. The vehicle stopped dead in its tracks.

Pastor turned to the driver with a relieved smile. Claudia tried to straighten herself up. The *taxista* drove on calmly. Pastor slapped him on the shoulder, dug a couple of twenty dollar bills out of his pocket and handed them to the driver.

"*Bien hecho, señor taxista,* well done."

"*Gracias, señor,*" the man said to the image in the rear view mirror, "*muchisimas gracias.*"

—

After the harrowing taxi ride, Pastor and Claudia checked in late at the Hotel Central in Villahermosa. They decided it would be safer to share a room and Pastor picked up a bottle of gin and some tonic at an attached bar to help them wind down from the recent excitement.

"Who were those people chasing us, John?" Claudia sat in a large chair in the middle of the room.

"I don't know. I thought you might have some idea." Pastor handed her a room temperature drink, then topped off his own. He walked over and sat on the edge of one of two beds in the room. "But it was too close a call for me. I've been having a lot of those lately. Way too many."

"I don't think, Juanito, that you are well liked here in Mexico."

"The taxi driver liked me."

"Of course, you gave him a week's pay for a tip."

"The man saved our lives."

"How many people are after you?"

"Right now, Claudia, I would say that the only person I know for sure isn't after me, is me."

"I'm not after you."

"Just my luck."

"I *have* you." Claudia stood up and began to unbutton her dress.

"Hmm," Pastor murmured.

"It's so hot here."

"It's almost spring." Pastor stood also. "The equinox is just around the corner. It gets hot around here from now on."

"I think I'll wash off in the shower." She winked.

"Can I help?" He stepped so close to her their lips nearly touched.

"Not just yet," she demurred.

Claudia brushed by him and went into the bathroom, leaving the door slightly open. Pastor couldn't resist a quick peek as she finished undressing and climbed into the shower. He whistled softly, then walked across the room and poured himself a tall shot of straight gin. Sipping on the drink, he went to the window to look out on the rain-glistened streets of Villahermosa. It was a quiet morning. After a few minutes, he set the drink down on the window sill, walked to the chair Claudia had been in and took off his shoes and then his shirt.

He heard her finish showering.

"Juanito," she called to him, "would you get me a towel? I have some soap in my eyes."

"With pleasure." He got up and headed to the bathroom.

Inside, he took a large towel from a rack by the sink and handed it to Claudia who reached for it from behind the shower curtain.

"*Gracias, guero*."

"*Guero*, you called me *guero*. That means blondie, right?"

"I don't mean it badly. It's a term of affection, too."

"Like *morena* for women."

"Like *morena* for women."

"Well, *morena*, can I help finish drying you off?"

"I'm almost done, thanks, but I would like a new drink."

While Pastor made Claudia and himself another drink, she stepped out of the shower wrapped only in the towel he had brought her. Returning with a drink in each hand, he offered one to her.

"Ah, that's good." She sipped the drink and sighed.

"It sure is." Pastor looked her over from head to toe.

She stood close to him and extended her glass.

He touched it with his. "*Salud, guapa*."

He moved up to her, face to face.

She set her drink down. "I'm getting sweaty again."

"Me, too."

They moved closer yet, almost, then finally kissing. They kissed slowly at first, lightly, then more passionately. Pastor reached down and loosened the towel. They continued kissing as the towel dropped from her and fell in a heap on the floor.

—

Chango Morales stood in front of a large window looking out from his expensively furnished home office. Reflected in the window he could see one of his big bodyguards standing beyond his paper-covered desk. Outside, he looked down upon the great city itself, Mexico City, awash in a sea of light. Chango held a phone in his left hand and spoke excitedly into it.

"Has Ortega reported in yet? Good. Did the parcel arrive safely? What? I can't hear you well. Repeat what you said. Two parcels? And? But they're okay? Excellent. Is everything prepared on that end?"

Chango turned away from the window and came out from behind the desk. He paced around the room, ignoring the bodyguard who impassively stared straight ahead.

"Tell Chuy not to let anything happen to our parcel. Is that clear? Okay. I'll be there as soon as I take care of some business here. Understood? All right. Now listen, once the arrangements have been made I want a full report on the second parcel. Chuy knows what to do. Okay. Make sure someone will be there to meet me. *Bueno. Hasta luego.*"

"Always a complication," Chango told the bodyguard after ending the call. "Remember that, *joven*. No matter how well you prepare for something, there's always another detail to consider."

The bodyguard nodded as if he understood Chango's complaint.

"I need to go downtown. Is the car ready?"

"*Sí, señor.*"

"Then, let's go. This thing is far from over."

The bodyguard stepped to one side and opened the office door for Chango. The ex-detective marched through it.

—

Pastor quietly dressed, making sure he did not wake Claudia. He took his .380 automatic from a small case and put it in a holster behind his back, then slipped on a light jacket. Tiptoeing past their bed, he stopped momentarily to look down at her. For a moment, he seemed mesmerized.

"*Nos vemos, morena,*" he whispered before slipping out of the hotel room, "see you, brown woman."

Outside he found a taxi that took him to an early opening rental car company and the town was barely stirring yet as he headed out on Route 186 in a relatively new Ford Fiesta. It was still early when he reached the Route 199 cut off to Palenque just before the little town of Catazajá.

As he neared Ciudad Palenque on 199, Pastor slowed up. It was going to be all intuition and guesswork from here. Up ahead he saw a *campesino* carrying a bundle of firewood on his back. He stopped the man and showed him the picture of Anne Martin. The man shook his head and Pastor continued on. Further on he spotted a young boy coming by on a bicycle. He flagged the boy down and again displayed the photo. The boy shrugged and hurriedly pedaled away.

Finally, Pastor found a small store just opening for the day. He parked and got out to stretch. A man, presumably the owner, was rolling up the store's metal front shutters. Pastor brought out the photo again and after a moment the man pointed down the road with hand signals indicating several turns.

"*Gracias, señor.*" Pastor produced several Mexican paper bills and offered them to the man. The man refused with a wave. Pastor shook the man's hand, jumped back in the Fiesta and drove off down the road.

He made the turns just as the storekeeper had indicated and as the road began to play out from one-lane blacktop to an unpaved trail, he pulled off to the side in a small clearing a few hundred yards from some small buildings. He got out and checked his .380. Locked and loaded. Re-holstering the weapon, he cautiously wound his way through the thick foliage toward the buildings.

As quietly as he could, he worked his way up beside the largest of the buildings and peered in a window. He could make out three or four men, one of whom looked to be a North American. One man rested in a hammock, while the others were on the floor in sleeping bags. There were at least two women as well, one of whom shared the hammock.

By one wall he saw several semi-automatic rifles and handguns lying about. On a large table in the middle of the room were several open bags, some of their contents spilled out. It didn't take a DEA agent to recognize a shipment of marijuana.

He took it all in, was so engrossed in observing the group and their things that he did not at first react to the sound of a door opening just around the corner of the building. When it rattled shut, he dropped down by the side of the house.

He carefully peeked around the corner to see who had come out. It was a girl. A disheveled, even dirty girl. He checked the picture he carried. There was no doubt.

Anne Martin.

She yawned, stretched, and walked a few yards away from the house. Pastor watched her as she slowly, even lazily strolled out into some nearby bushes. She went behind them, lifted her peasant skirt, bent slightly and urinated on the ground.

While the girl relieved herself, Pastor warily, but quickly, came up behind her. When she was done, she wiped herself with a Kleenex and stood up. As she did, Pastor grabbed her, putting his left hand over her mouth. At first she seemed to think it was one of the men playing with her but when Pastor tightened his grip on her mouth she began to struggle. Pastor grabbed her thin body with his right hand and held her firmly. She continued to struggle but he was able to control her.

"Shh," he whispered, "quiet, honey. We're going to take a little ride. Your family will be real glad to see you."

He drug the struggling girl down the road toward his car. About halfway there she temporarily broke free, kicking him in the shins and elbowing him in the stomach to get loose.

"Paco! Eddie!" Her shrill voice cracked the quiet morning air. "*Ayudame!* Help me!"

"Damn you." He fought to regain control of the squirming girl.

They fought briefly then he drew back his right hand and delivered a hard punch to the girl's jaw. She dropped limply into his arms. He tossed her over his shoulders like a bag of grain and ran to the car as fast as his load and aging legs would let him. Behind, he heard sounds of movement inside the bigger house, then voices crying out.

"What was that? Hey, Paco, did you hear that?" A male voice, *gringo.*

"It sounded like Ana, man." Another male, Mexican, responded.

"*Que pasa, que haces?* What's happening? What are you doing?" A Mexican woman.

"*Dame la pistola, vamos.*"

"Grab your shit, man, there's something going down outside."

Pastor rushed toward the car, the girl dangling over his back, her head limply bouncing against his body. As he tossed the girl in the rider's seat and hurried back around to the driver's side, several young men appeared up the road, guns flashing in the sunlight. They fired wildly in Pastor's direction but their shots fell well away from his car.

He cranked up the Fiesta, burnt a U-turn, mud and grass flying, and headed back down the road away from his pursuers. He could hear rounds from a high-powered rifle whizzing by, then a round shattered the back window sending glass flying all over the interior of the vehicle. He instinctively ducked and when he did the car slid into a mud hole and temporarily stalled. Frantically trying to restart the engine, he heard the pursuers approaching, their shots honing in.

"Son of a bitch. *Start*, you bastard."

Just as the rounds were really zeroing in, the engine turned over and it lurched forward out of the mud hole.

"Go baby, go." He leaned out the window and fired several rounds back at the pursuers.

In the rear view mirror, he saw a shot had hit one of the men in the leg and the man dropped to the side of the road, his weapon bouncing into the tall grass. Suddenly, Pastor saw another of the men fall behind him, then heard unexpected gunfire coming from the jungle to his left.

"What the hell?"

Again looking back, he saw the pursuers break off the chase to seek shelter in the jungle. The sound of exchanged gunfire briefly filled the air, then lessened, and stopped.

"Jesus Christ, who is that? What's going on, now?" He floored the Fiesta. "I'm outta here."

—

José Matanza hammered whiskey from a large glass while Sonny Boston, sober and stressed out, paced back and forth on the thick carpet behind a large wet bar in a back room of Matanza's Mexico City home. In one corner, two of Matanza's bodyguards impassively watched the proceedings.

"Damn it, José," Boston could no longer contain himself, "now you've lost Anne and the stupid detective."

"*Calmate*, Sonny. I have my people on the *drogistas* right now. They will find them, don't worry."

"Your people. Your people. A bunch of incompetent fools, if you ask me. Led by a bigger one."

"Don't ever talk to me that way again, Sonny," Matanza's eyes flared. He slammed down his drink and pointed menacingly. "This is my home, my country. Never do that again."

"Don't forget who you're working for, José," Boston countered, "I won't tolerate threats. From you or your men. You screwed this up and now by God you're going to straighten it up."

"We will get the trail again." Matanza backed off at Boston's display of authority. "Very soon. My people are looking right now. I promise you we'll find them."

"Whatever you do." Boston took a deep breath. "Keep your men back. I don't want Anne hurt. The equinox is only a few days away and if your information is correct, she and her bunch and probably Pastor now, too, will be at Chichen Itza."

"We are certain they intend to do something that day. My source is reliable."

"Is this the same source that told you Pastor, the "stupid" *gringo*, always worked alone?"

"*Mira*, Sonny, we do not know who helped him get out of Palenque. But there was a woman, and others. We don't know who yet."

"Well, find out. And keep your men on it. But don't interfere any more. It's getting too close to the payoff."

"As you wish."

"It is my wish, my command."

"It will come out okay, Sonny. You'll see. We have it under control. We only have to follow, watch, and jump at the right moment."

"See that it happens." Boston pointed at Matanza. "No more screw-ups."

—

Pastor backtracked toward Route 186 to begin the long trek to the Yucatan Coast. With each passing mile he became more relaxed, checked the rear view mirror less often. The girl regained consciousness slowly, rubbing her bruised jaw from Pastor's blow. A good half hour passed before she spoke.

"Who are you?"

"Name's John Pastor."

"What do you want? What are you going to do to me?"

"I'm not going to do anything to you, Miss Martin, I'm going to take you back to the States, as soon as it's safe that is."

"You a cop?"

"No, I work alone."

"You're a lousy PI?"

"That's right, Miss Martin, a lousy PI."

She sized Pastor up with a long look.

"Call me, Anne," her tone softened, became almost friendly.

"All right… Anne."

"You can untie my hands you know. I'm not dangerous."

"I will. Later."

"Where are we going?" The girl looked out the window, saw a Route 186 sign flash by.

"To a friend's place. Where we'll both be safe. I hope."

"Where at?"

"You'll see. It's a nice place. By the beach. Quiet and out of the way."

"I guess, you're not such a bad guy, then, are you?" The girl shifted in her seat toward Pastor, her skirt hiking well up her leg to reveal a slender, dark thigh. Pastor saw and scratched his chin.

"I'm just doing my job, Miss…."

"Anne."

"Anne. Somebody, I assume your family, wants you to come back home. That's what I'm being paid for, that's what we're going to do."

"I understand, John." The girl slid over as close as she could get to him. He could feel the warmth of her body next to him. "You're a man of action. I like a man of action. They're the only kind I like."

"Why don't you…. whoa there!" Pastor felt her reach inside his jacket.

He grabbed her hands, still tied together, with his right and steered with the left. The car veered back and forth across the road as the girl kicked and bit Pastor until he was forced to hit her solidly with his right forearm. She banged against the rider side door, eyes blazing with anger.

"Damn girl, stop. You're going to get us killed."

"You'll never get me back to the States, you old shit. Paco and the others will get you, they'll be coming for me right now."

"No doubt. Real tough guys, huh? Last I saw of them they were pinned down back at your little jungle Shangri-la like a pack of little punks."

"Screw you, jerk." The girl straightened her clothes and wiped a trickle of blood from the corner of her mouth.

"Yeah, well, get in line."

Pastor drove the Fiesta on through the Mexican countryside. He didn't check the rear view mirror much anymore. He had all he could handle right there inside the car with him.

—

The sun rose powerfully from the Mexican Caribbean, its potent rays bathing the verdant Yucatan terrain and Pastor's vehicle in a breathtaking gold. He lowered his visor to partially block out the light. The girl, in obvious physical discomfort, jerkily awakened. Her eyes were puffy and red and she had begun to sniffle—nearly a day away now from whatever steady diet of whatever she was used to ingesting. Pastor, yawning and stiff from the long drive, watched Anne as she shifted around in the seat.

"Damn you, you said you'd untie me," she sniffed. "It's not funny, damn it. My head hurts. I feel like hell."

"You'll be all right."

"What do you know?"

"Maybe more than you think."

"Right." She awkwardly pulled her legs up in the seat and leaned against the door. "Where the hell are we?"

"Just past Tulum. You should see it sometime. Right by the ocean so you get a great view and a cool breeze."

"You would know about ruins, being one yourself."

"A little touchy, are we this morning?"

"Where are you taking me, Pastor?"

"Not John anymore?"

"Just tell me, please."

"Some place where you can dry out."

"Dry out? Jesus, where do you come from, the 1940s? Who's paying you to kidnap me?"

"I'm not kidnapping you. I'm hauling your young ass back to the States. As soon as you get squared away and cleaned up some."

"I bet you'd like to do the cleaning up part, too, huh, with my young ass?"

"You're a real badass, aren't you?"

"And rich, too. I'll give you money to let me go. Is that what turns you on? How much are you getting for this? I'll pay you twice as much to let me go."

"Right. Listen, sweetie, I've been on a wild goose chase all over this country looking for you. I'm not letting you go."

"Paco will never let you get away with this. It's nearly the equinox."

"What? What did you say?"

"Nothing."

"The equinox. The spring equinox? What in the hell's that mean? No, please, don't explain. I've lived down here for God knows how long and all of a sudden I don't understand anything anymore. Everything's a goddamn mystery and I don't get any clues."

"Just forget it."

"Great."

For a few moments, then, they were quiet. Pastor guided the Fiesta along the narrow roadway while the girl resumed watching the passing land. Just after they passed a sign for Playa del Carmen and Cancun, she tried again.

"My father will pay you three times, no, four times what you're being paid, John, really."

"The rich Mr. Martin, ey?"

"That's not his name. His name is Boston."

"What? Boston? Did you say Boston?"

"Yes, Francis Boston. He's a big—"

"Land developer in Arizona," Pastor finished her sentence.

"Then you've heard of him. He's wealthy. He'll pay you to let me go."

"Dead—or alive?"

"What's that supposed to mean?"

"Nothing."

"What are you saying?"

"Forget it. I'm just really tired."

"You don't think I am?"

"Ah, thank God," Pastor said, "the turnoff at last."

He slowed the vehicle at an unmarked intersection with a Pemex gas station and attached convenience store on the left and a dirt road on the right. He turned down the dirt road.

"Where is this? Where are we going?"

"To an old friend's. You'll be safe here. You can relax."

"I *am* relaxed. Why are you telling me to relax?"

"Never mind." Pastor maneuvered the Fiesta down the road toward the coast. "Just take it easy."

"I want to know what you meant by that crack about my father. What do you mean dead or alive?"

Within sight of the beach, Pastor pulled the car into a sandy driveway leading from the road to a small house hidden behind a small stand of trees and shrubs. An older Mexican man came out of the house as they parked. He was medium-height and build, with graying dark hair. When he saw Pastor he smiled.

"Sorry," Pastor said, "forget what I said. Here's Hector."

"Your accomplice in kidnapping."

"My old friend. One of the kindest men I've ever known."

"Well, isn't that wonderful."

"I'll untie your hands when we get settled." Pastor climbed out of the car and walked toward his old friend. "Hector, it's great to see you again."

—

Pastor relaxed in a lawn chair on the porch looking toward the beach. The sun was low in the western sky behind and the area was bathed in soft light. The back screen door opened and Hector walked out. He slid another lawn chair beside Pastor.

"How is she?"

"She is sleeping. I gave her three pills. She'll be okay."

"Good. Listen, Hector. I'm sorry to bust in on you like this."

"No problem, it's good to see you again, amigo."

"Same here, pal. I would have let you know if I could."

"No worries." Hector held out a small bottle of tequila. "Want to walk on the beach?"

"What about the girl?"

"She's out. No problem. I locked the house."

The men shared hits from the bottle as they ambled along to the beach. Once there they turned right, to the south, and walked casually at the edge of the water.

"What will you do with the girl?" Hector handed Pastor the tequila.

"Probably fly her out of Cancun in a few days." He took a drink and handed the bottle back to Hector. "After things have settled down some here. I'd like to lay low for a couple of days, if it's all right."

"My home is yours."

"Thank you, Hector, but are you sure it's okay? It could get dangerous. I hope we don't have any trouble but this girl's friends are nasty characters."

"Where did you find her?"

"Palenque."

"That's a long way away."

"It's the strangest case I've ever had," Pastor said. "Too many things have happened. I'm not used to it. It wasn't like this, even on the border. Not even close."

"Sounds bad."

"The worst part—besides being shot at, run off the road, and arrested—is that this started off as a simple missing person case. But now there seems to be a whole lot of people involved and a bunch of loose ends I can't tie together. Just when I think I have it sort of figured out, something else comes along to muddy up the water."

"I don't know."

"Must sound stupid to you, huh?"

"No," Hector said, "more like complicated."

"Yeah, and I think there are maybe two or three sides in all this, too. And they seem to be switching among themselves with me in the middle not even knowing what I'm in the middle of. In Palenque, somebody showed up and helped me escape by fighting the girl's boyfriends. I don't have any idea who that was."

"Well, whoever they were, they helped," Hector said. "That's all that matters and whatever it is, it will soon be over. You can take the girl back to wherever she belongs and that will be that. Here, have another drink."

Pastor took a long belt of the tequila and handed it back. He stood for a moment and looked out at the sea. "Beautiful, isn't it? I love the Yucatan."

"Especially this time of year is good, not yet too hot."

"Speaking of time of the year, do you know if the spring equinox has some special meaning out here or something? Anything unusual you're aware of?"

"Spring equi....?"

"Equinox. The day spring begins."

"I don't know. It's just spring, uh— no, no, of course. It's Chichen Itza. There's a... a *thing* at Chichen Itza. The god Kukulcan, Quetzalcoatl, returns."

"What? Some god returns? From where?"

"On the pyramid El Castillo at nightfall." Hector told the legend in between drinks of tequila. "The shadows play down the steps of the pyramid and Quetzalcoatl, the plumed serpent, the eternal god, returns to earth. That is the story."

"And this happens on the equinox."

"The first day of spring."

"Hector, now how about this? Have you ever heard of the *Piedra de Sangre?*"

"*Como no*, everyone in Mexico has heard of the bloodstone. Why?"

"Well, I don't know too much about it, only that it was stolen a long time ago and it's worth a lot."

"Yes, it is without price. The *arqueologistas* discovered it early in the century at Teotihuacan," Hector elaborated. "It is an ancient knife used for sacrifices. A long blade of stone and a jade handle, with a ruby on top. There are pictures of it in the museum of anthropology."

"That was where it was stolen from, right? And back in the 30s as I remember. I talked to an old professor in Cuernavaca about it."

"There was a cult in the 30s, Juanito, they worshipped Quetzalcoatl."

"The plumed serpent god."

"*La serpienta enplumada*. Yes. These people were also patriots. They loved Mexico and her Indian past and did not believe it should be destroyed. They wanted the ruins closed to all but Mexicans. It is said they returned the bloodstone and other treasures they stole to the ruins themselves."

"Then the bloodstone," Pastor surmised, "should be somewhere in Teotihuacan. Like old Professor Garcia suggested. Maybe the old guy wasn't so senile after all."

"Professor Garcia?"

"The old professor I saw in Cuernavaca. He was this girl's teacher. It's another long story. No wonder somebody wanted to chase me away from Teotihuacan. The treasure probably really was there."

"Maybe not," Hector said. "In the late 30s, during the time of Lazaro Cardenas, the cult was in— infiltrated and broken up by the federal police. The leader of the cult was killed at Palenque and some of the treasures they had stolen were found there. They found out the group had hidden treasures all over the country in different ruins."

"Say, Hector." Pastor paused in their walk and looked back inland. "We better get back to the house. The last thing I want to do is lose our guest."

"Let's take this little trail over here." Hector pointed to a narrow path away from the beach. "It'll get us back to the house quick."

"Good idea, man." Pastor followed Hector down the trail to the house. "There's no place for her to go but it's better to keep her in sight. She's valuable property. We can hash out all this crap about the bloodstone later. This girl is my own bloodstone for now."

—

Claudia sat on a bench beneath a carefully and symmetrically trimmed tree in the park that is the centerpiece of Merida's *jardín* or town plaza, reading a local newspaper. From across the plaza she watched a well-groomed older man slowly walk toward her. When he reached the bench, he sat down without speaking, pulled out a pipe, filled it with tobacco and lit it. Smoke from the pipe curled up into the air and pushed by a light breeze floated by Claudia. She folded the newspaper and set it on the bench beside her.

"Thank you for meeting me here." She looked straight ahead.

"I'm not happy with what I hear, Claudia."

"And good day to you, too, Inspector."

"I'm sorry, child." The Inspector did not smile. "As I get older there seems to be less and less time for formality."

"Of course." Claudia patted him on the hand. "Forgive me."

"I just don't want to see you get hurt."

"I know, and I thank you for that, but you've got to trust me. I know what I'm doing."

"Let's hope so, Claudia," the Inspector began but was cut off by the loud approach of a small local band, "for your sake…."

The band stopped several yards from the bench and began to play a raucous, Mexican military-sounding song.

The Inspector motioned with his pipe. "Let's take a walk."

They rose and Claudia slipped her arm through his as they walked across the park.

"Rumors have it, my dear," the Inspector resumed the conversation when they were well away from the band and near an open air café on the other side of the plaza, "that you've lost yourself a *gringo*. Is that true? And why wouldn't you want him to stay lost?"

"I have. And no, I don't want him to stay lost. I need him."

"Need him? Look around you, there are hundreds of fine young men here. *Yucatecos*. Why would you need a *gringo?*"

"You are being dense on purpose. I don't need him that way."

"Again." The Inspector raised an eyebrow as they stopped beneath a large shade tree at the edge of the plaza and turned to look at each other. "That is not what the rumors say."

"You must have gotten this from Sergio in Villahermosa. He never knows when to keep his nose out of other people's business."

"You must be more discreet, my dear."

"I am only myself," Claudia said with a little heat. "It's all I can be. All I know how to be."

"All right, dear. Don't take offense. I am just worried about you. You've been like a daughter to me."

"And I love you for it. But you must let me be a woman. I am one, you know."

"Only a fool or a blind man could think otherwise."

"Flatterer." Claudia kissed the Inspector on the forehead.

"So what is it you want of me, then?" He sighed. "To use my contacts in this god-forsaken jungle land and find this gringo of yours, against my better judgment?"

"Yes, please. He's good at getting lost most of the time but there may be others who are not as easily fooled as I. And they will certainly not find his disappearing act amusing."

"He's important to your work, then?"

"Yes, very much so."

"I'll make inquiries—quietly. I won't endanger your *gringo* more."

"Thank you, Inspector. You're a wonderful man."

"But one," the Inspector said as they continued their walk, blending in with the sights and sounds of the busy, colorful plaza, "thirty years older than he wishes to be."

—

Late in the evening, Hector semi-dozed on a couch while Pastor, sitting in a chair across the room, read from a small book about the ruins at Chichen Itza. He heard a shuffling noise and was about to put the book down when Anne came into the kitchen yawning and stretching. Pastor closed the book and laid it face down on the table.

"Well, good evening, Anne. Feeling any better?"

"Yes." She rubbed her wrists, wiggled her fingers. "Especially now that I'm not tied up anymore."

"You stay mellow," Pastor told her, "you stay untied."

"Would you like something to eat, miss?" Hector had roused from his rest. "Maybe some fruit?"

Hector went into the small, adjoining kitchen area and began rustling through some paper sacks. Anne sat down in the chair Hector vacated. She and Pastor exchanged expressionless looks. In a few minutes, Hector came back with a plate full of fruit and a small roll of string cheese and handed them to Anne.

She dug into the fruit, hungrily downing a banana and an orange. After the fruit, she jerked short slices of cheese off the roll.

"What?" She paused in mid-bite, seeing the men watching her. "You never see anybody eat before?"

"Maybe not like that," Pastor said.

"Is there anything to drink besides water?"

"I got a couple of beers," Hector offered, "but they're al tiempo."

"Room temp is okay by me."

"Okay."

Hector walked over to a small ice chest, took out a beer and brought it to Anne.

"Thanks."

"*De nada.*"

Hector took another chair beside Pastor.

"No wilting lily, huh?" Pastor said, when the girl nearly chugged the beer.

"What's that supposed to mean?" Anne wiped her mouth with the back of her hand.

"Nothing. Just you're no rookie."

"I been around."

Anne saw Pastor's jacket on the other end of the couch. It was open enough for her to notice the pack of cigarettes.

"Uh-huh." Pastor followed the movement of her eyes.

"How about one of your cigarettes?"

"You don't need to smoke, not a young woman like you."

"You're so full of it, John."

"So, I'm John again, now, huh?"

Anne snorted and looked away.

"I thought you quit a long time ago, Juan," Hector said. "When did you start again?"

"I didn't. I just bought them on a whim. Don't know why. I guess I was feeling low."

"You're a strange bird, Pastor," Anne said.

"It has been mentioned to me before."

"Well, what happens next? How long do you keep me cooped up here?"

"There's nowhere to run, Anne, if that's what you're thinking."

"I wasn't."

"Good. Just take it easy and when you feel better we'll catch a plane back to the States."

Anne fell silent, her eyes scanning the room. She and Pastor simultaneously focused on a wall telephone. The girl quickly looked away. Pastor glanced at Hector.

"All right." Anne stretched elaborately. "I want to rest some more now. Good night, captors."

"Good night, free girl," Pastor countered.

"*Buenas noches, señorita,*" Hector said.

Anne gave them a cute little wave as she left the room.

"Crap, Hector, man," Pastor said when he heard the girl shut the door to her room. "That phone. When did you get that damn phone?"

"*Tranquilate.*" Hector raised and lowered his right hand. "*Calma.* It's okay, *amigo.* It doesn't work. The only phone around here is down at the station on the highway."

"Whew." Pastor breathed a sigh of relief. "Thank God for bad phone service in the Yucatan." His brow suddenly furrowed. "We shouldn't have left her alone, untied. She could have slipped away."

"Don't worry, John." Hector reassured his friend. "No way, she was too out of it. And you saw how she looked at this phone. If she'd got out, she wouldn't be checking it out like that."

"I don't know. She's been around, Hector, especially for someone her age. This girl is more trouble than I bargained for. More than she's worth."

"Ah, forget about it. She didn't leave."

"I hope not. I sure as hell hope not."

—

Paco and Eddie, both wearing sidearms, had holed up in a ratty hotel in Ciudad Cancun far from the wealthy watering holes of the city's touristy hotel row. Eddie lay on one bed next to a large, open travel bag while Paco paced by a window, smoking a cigarette and taking an occasional swig from a bottle of mezcal. Through the window, they heard popular Mexican music coming from a nearby *cantina.*

Suddenly there was a knock on the door, timid at first, then repeated, but louder. Eddie sprang off the bed, drawing his pistol. Paco set the mezcal down and pulled out his pistol as well. Eddie moved up to the side of the front door while Paco went into the tiny bathroom and stood just out of sight, pistol raised at shoulder height.

"Who is it?" Eddie asked. The knock came again. "*Adelante,* come in."

The door opened slowly and a short, stocky man, missing several of his front teeth, warily entered the room. He raised his hands fearfully when he saw Eddie's pistol and higher yet when Paco emerged from the bathroom. Eddie frisked the man, while Paco covered him.

"Who are you?" Eddie demanded.

"I— I can help you," the man stammered.

"Who says we need help?"

"Did Martinez send you?" Paco said.

The man looked around nervously but was silent.

"He's a fuckin' freelancer, Paco." Eddie put his pistol against the man's head. "He's peddlin' info. I oughta kill you, you slimy weasel."

The man cringed.

Paco intervened. "Let's see what he has to say. "He's got…uh, initiative."

Paco and Eddie laughed.

"*Yo se que ustedes*...." the man began.

"*En Ingles, hombre*," Paco said, "*Ingles*."

"I know you lost something. I can help you find what you're looking for."

"Shit." Eddie snorted.

"Let's say we did lose something," Paco said. "How can you help us? And why would you?"

The man looked longingly at the big, open bag on the bed. There were several clear plastic bags sticking out of it. Paco noticed.

"Go ahead, Eduardo." he pointed at the bag. "For our new friend."

Eddie walked to the bed and extracted a baggie full of white powder. The man's eyes lit up. Eddie opened the top drawer of a bedside table and pulled out a Bible. He ripped a page out and poured two lines of cocaine on the page, then set it on the table. The man crossed himself but walked over to the table and snorted the cocaine loudly. He rubbed it off his nose and wiped his gums with the residue. Paco handed him the bottle of mezcal. The man took a drink and grinned. He only had about three teeth in his mouth. Eddie turned away.

"What do you have for us?" Paco asked.

The informant grinned stupidly.

"Jesus," Eddie said, "coke ain't enough for this pig. Dust him, Paco."

"Pay the man, Eddie."

"Pay him? For what? Screw him."

"Go on."

"Shit."

Eddie reluctantly pulled some bills out of the travel bag. He handed the man a U.S. twenty. Paco signaled for more. Eddie gave the man another twenty, then two tens.

"*Muy bien, amigos, muchas gracias*," the man dug around in his pants and came up with a piece of paper, which he handed to Paco and Eddie to read.

"Very good, thank you, friend." Paco folded the paper and put it in his shirt pocket. "Eddie, give the man a nickel bag to go."

"Christ almighty." Eddie reached in the bag again and came up with a small plastic bag, which he tossed to the informant. "Now get the hell out. *Adios*. We're done here."

"*Adios, señores.*" The man backed out the door. "*Muchas gracias*."

"What in the hell did you do that for?" Eddie confronted Paco when the man was gone. "You gave him way too much, man."

Paco signaled toward the door with his head. Eddie grinned.

"Gotcha, brother. Right on."

It only took Eddie about five minutes to find the man. He was at a small kiosk just outside a narrow, dark alley buying a bottle of tequila and a pack of cigarettes. Collecting his purchases, the man stumbled into the alley. He stopped to open the pack of cigarettes, then searched his pockets for a light. Without warning, Eddie suddenly appeared, holding a cigarette lighter. The cigarette fell from the man's mouth. Eddie took the pack from him and pulled out cigarettes for each of them. Eddie lit his own cigarette, then had to hold the man's shaking hands to light his.

"We didn't get a chance to thank you properly for helping us before." Eddie said. "You left a little too soon."

"No problem," the man said. "It's okay. I gotta go now."

"Again so soon?" Eddie stepped toward the man, who squealed, turned and ran. But not far. Paco was waiting at the top of the alley.

"*Ay, Dios mio*," the man moaned.

"That's right, *amigo*." Paco tightened a silencer to the barrel of the pistol he held. "Pray to your god."

"*No, señor, por favor, no*."

"*Adios, maricón.*"

Paco fired twice. One round hit the man in the chest, the second splattered his forehead into the alley. Eddie walked over and dug through the man's clothes.

"Hell, the bastard already spent ten dollars."

"A wasteful man."

"Yeah, really wasteful." Eddie said.

At the sound of a distant siren, they hustled out the other end of the alley and vanished into the dark Cancun night.

—

Pastor tossed and turned under the mosquito netting of his bed in the throes of a bad dream. His face was wet with sweat and he flailed his arms about and cried out softly.

"No, no, watch out. Karen, Amy. No. Look out. Ahh… Matanza, you bastard, you killed them. Karen. Amy. Help… *No!*"

Suddenly he sat bolt upright, wide awake. "Jesus Christ."

The house was quiet and through an open window he could hear a light breeze blowing through the trees and the low lapping of the ocean onto the beach. He lay back down then, rehashing the murders of his wife and daughter years ago when he was stationed in Texas along the Mexican border. He'd had the nightmare many times since. He could never stop their deaths and he could never forget or forgive himself. Finally, sometime near dawn, exhausted from regret and remorse, he was able to drift back off into a quiet, dreamless slumber.

Early the next morning with Pastor still sleeping under the mosquito netting, the door to his room opened and Anne quietly slipped in. She wore a towel draped over wet undergarments. She went silently to the bed, sat on the edge of it and pulled back the netting.

"What the….?" Pastor woke with a start. "What's going on?"

"It's just me, Anne."

"What are you doing? Where've you been?"

"Just to the water. It was so refreshing."

"Where's Hector?"

"Relax." Anne scooted a little closer to Pastor, "He kept an eye on me like a good boy."

"What is it you want?"

"Nothing. I was just wondering about what's going to happen, that's all."

"Well, it's really simple, Anne." Pastor sat up in bed, pulling the sheets around his midsection. "In a day or so we hop a plane to the States and you go back to your family."

"To my stepdad, you mean."

"Whoever."

"I'm sorry I've been difficult. It's been tough down here."

"Yeah, I can see how it could be."

"But I feel much better now."

Anne took off the towel, ran it through her hair and then dropped it beside the bed.

"You look better. Healthier."

"You think so?"

"Yes. Underneath that tough facade you like to adopt, you're really a pretty young woman."

"You say that like you're some old grandpa or something."

"That's how I feel most of the time."

"But you're not. You're really still young."

"I wish I felt that way."

"I could make you feel that way."

"I'm sure you could."

"Wouldn't you like that, John?" She let her right arm lightly drop far down onto Pastor's stomach. He flinched slightly.

"I don't think I better answer that."

"It's okay if you do."

He leaned away from her. "There's one thing I have to ask you, though."

"What's that, John?"

"What were you talking about the equinox the other day? Does it have something to do with the bloodstone? The god coming back and showing up at Chichen Itza?"

For the briefest of moments Pastor saw in the girl's eyes a strange look, perhaps a mixture of excitement and dread, but she shut that window just as quickly as it had opened.

"Let's not talk about that." She leaned toward him again.

"The spring equinox is in a couple of days. What's going down?"

"They do that equinox thing every year at Chichen Itza," she said. "Let's talk about it later. Right now I'm interested in something else."

Reaching behind her back, she unsnapped her bra and let it fall to the floor. Pastor drank in her naked upper body, then pulled her, willingly, to him. For several moments they locked in a series of breathless embraces until he rolled her over onto her back. He began to take off his t-shirt but she reached up for him.

"Just a minute." He broke from her hold.

When he did free himself he saw through a window, beyond some tall plants beside the house, movement, then two men sneaking up on the house. Feeling Pastor tense, the girl tried to regain his attention.

"Come on, baby, please. Let's do it."

"Goddamn it." Pastor pushed her away. "Turn loose."

He leaped out of bed in his shorts and t-shirt, grabbed his pants and at the same time pulled his pistol out of one of the pants pockets.

"Eddie! Paco!" Anne stood on the bed and screamed. "He's in here."

"You dirty little bitch, when did you get out?"

"You're so bad, Pastor, I've gotten out of here twice."

"You stupid little girl."

"You're the stupid one. You'll never get me out of here now. They'll kill you first."

"We'll see about that." Pastor drug her off the bed. He looked around the room, saw a closet and hauled her to it. "Hector," he called out a warning, "*pues, hay bandidos, cuidado.* Bandits, look out."

"*Maldita sea,*" he heard Hector from the living room. "*Que mala onda.* This is bad shit."

Pastor pushed the girl, kicking and screaming, into the closet. He found his belt and ran it through the handles of the closet, secured it, then shoved a chair against it. With her at least temporarily locked up, he went to the window and with pistol in hand carefully looked outside.

There was no one in sight.

"*Donde estan?*" Hector came into the room with an old, five-shot clip, bolt action rifle.

"Hey, *gringo*," they heard one of the men outside call, "let the woman go and we don't kill you." At the sound of the bandit's voice, the girl repeatedly banged against the inside of the closet door and cried out.

"Paco, Eddie, I'm here. Come get me."

"Not gonna happen, Paco," Pastor yelled, "she stays with me. Watch for Eddie, the *gringo*, Hector."

Pastor jerked his thumb at the door.

"*Bueno*." Hector turned, rifle at the ready.

"You let her go, old man," Paco called back, "or we're coming in."

"Come on." Pastor punctuated his answer by firing several rounds out the window. "We love visitors."

His fire was immediately met by a fierce retaliation from Paco. Hector and Pastor ducked down as wood and glass sprayed around the room. While they were hunkered down, Eddie suddenly appeared in the doorway.

"Die, mothers." He cranked off several wild rounds.

"*Híjole*." Hector hurriedly worked the bolt action. He fired quickly, accurately. Eddie dropped to the floor dead, his pistol rattling across the room.

"Juanito, you okay?"

"Damn it." Pastor held his upper left arm near the shoulder where one of Eddie's bullets had found its mark. Hector rushed to his side. "I'm all right. I think it just went through. I can still move it."

"We gotta get the other one." Hector again worked the bolt on his rifle. "Son of a bitch caught me off guard."

"Go out back." Pastor motioned with his pistol. "I'm going out the side."

Hector gingerly stepped over Eddie's motionless body as he exited the room. Pastor quickly went through a side door. Except for a light breeze playing in the trees and the sound of the distant surf, it was perfectly quiet outside.

Pastor made his way around the house until he was near the front door. He heard a thudding sound from within the house and pushed himself against the outside wall. After a moment, he edged onto the small front porch and slowly opened the door, pistol aimed into the shaded light of the indoors.

Inside, he carefully went down a short hall and turned to his right. In that moment, directly in front of him, framed in an opposite doorway, was Paco. He stood over Hector's prone body. In a moment that seemed in eternal slow motion, Paco turned and he and Pastor faced each other. For what seemed minutes but was only seconds they froze in time.

Then suddenly they reacted.

"You're dusted, *gringo*."

Paco fired as fast as he could pull the trigger. Pastor returned fire, again and again. Then there was the unmistakable thump of a body hitting the floor in free fall.

"Paco? Eddie?" Anne's muffled cry came from the closet. "Come get me."

A large hand pulled the chair away from the door and then unhooked the belt lock. Anne pushed the door open and looked up. Pastor stood before her, blood from his earlier wound staining his t-shirt.

"Sorry, sweetie," he said, "your pals couldn't make it." He pulled Anne out of the closet. She cried but offered no resistance. "Let's go, girl."

"Damn you," she whimpered.

"Shut up." Pastor put his pistol against the girl's temple. She cringed. "Just shut the hell up and tell me, now, about Chichen Itza."

"Go to hell," she sobbed. "Murderer."

Pastor grabbed her by the hair and drug her into the next room, where a dazed Hector leaned against a chair, rubbing the back of his head. Paco's bloody body lay on the floor.

"You okay, Hector?" Pastor came up to his friend, still holding onto the squirming girl.

"I'll be okay. The *cabrón* hit me in the head."

"That's the last time he'll do that," Pastor said grimly.

"Bastard," Anne cried. "You killed him. You filthy bastard."

"No more crap, little girl." Pastor twisted her arm behind her back. "Tell me what's up at Chichen Itza or I'll break your damned arm."

"There's supposed to be a sign." Anne continued to struggle. "A light or something that points to a big stone at the base of *El Castillo*."

"The big pyramid at Chichen Itza? What kind of light?"

"I don't know." Anne grimaced against Pastor's tight grip. "When the serpent comes down the pyramid on the first day of spring there's supposed to be a sign that shows where the bloodstone's buried. That's all I know, let me go."

"Hector." Pastor eased his grip slightly on the girl. "Can you watch her for a couple of days? Maybe take her to your family place in Merida?"

"I think so, Juan. It should be okay. I can check."

"You'll have to keep her under guard all the time," Pastor warned. "I mean don't ever let her out of your sight until I come for her. Never leave her alone, understand? You or somebody you trust has to watch her all the time."

"*Entiendo*. We can do it. But what about you, you will need me, no? Let me come with you to Chichen Itza."

"No, man, you nearly bought it today as it is. You've done enough out here. All I need is for you to watch the girl. She might end up being my only ticket out of all this."

"All right, my friend, but be careful. This bloodstone business seems to claim many sacrifices."

"Don't worry," Pastor said. "I don't plan on being the next one."

—

Pastor, a bandage covering the wound on his left arm, mingled with the throng of people gathered before the pyramid El Castillo at sundown, waiting for the moment when the lighting would make it appear that the feathered serpent god, Quetzalcoatl or Kukulcan, was returning to earth. He pushed his way through the crowd as close to the pyramid base as he could get and waited for the anticipated moment.

Finally the play of light and shadow on the pyramid steps was just right and the stairs seemed to come alive, undulating down to a carved stone head of the plumed serpent at the base of the pyramid. Pastor watched in awe until the light struck a slick stone in the eye of the serpent head and a thin yellow beam was for just the briefest of seconds refracted to a huge stone at the base of the pyramid. Pastor barely stifled a small cry of excitement, a cry lost in the general murmuring of the crowd which was still focused on the serpentine apparition and not looking for the minute sign that he saw. With a smile playing on his lips, he drifted back into the crowd and out of sight.

Early next morning before the ruins were overrun by tourists, Pastor returned to *El Castillo* with a small, collapsible shovel surreptitiously hidden away in a woven bag. Keeping an eye out for security, he located the large stone highlighted the night before and began to dig around it. Carefully excavating soil beside the stone, his shovel hit something solid. He continued digging with his hands and in a few nervous moments extracted a thick piece of folded cloth. Barely able to restrain himself, he peeled back the cloth to reveal, at long last, the bloodstone.

"My God." He knocked dirt and lint off the stone blade and rubbed the jade handle and large, rectangular inlaid ruby. "It is real."

While he was admiring the stone, a shadow crossed in front of him on the pyramid. He froze, then reached for his pistol tucked in his belt beneath the light jacket he wore. The sound of a familiar voice halted him in mid-action.

"Don't do it, my friend."

"Chango!" Pastor turned to see his trusted ally aiming a pistol right at him. He reholstered his own.

"Greetings, *amigo.*" Chango did not lower his pistol.

"What are you doing here?"

"Saving your life, Juanito."

"You have a funny way of going about it." He pointed at Chango's pistol.

"Don't worry, this is merely a precaution."

"You been hanging back all this time, Chango? Since the beginning?"

"I was trying to protect you, Juanito. That's why I sent you to the old professor. I knew he was a dead end. But you wouldn't stop there."

"How was I supposed to know he was a red herring? And who were you protecting me from?"

"The big people."

"Matanza and Boston?"

"When you came to see me again at Chapultepec Park," Chango ignored the questions, "I sent you to Monte Alban, again to protect you."

"Protect me? They tried to kill me there. This is bullshit, Chango. You were setting me up."

"I admit I thought it was all silly at first about the bloodstone, another of our legends, nothing more. But when I found out the big boys were really trying to stop you and that they believed the bloodstone was real and hidden somewhere, and that it was priceless, then I decided to help you."

"Help me?"

"Yes, to help you find the girl and the treasure. Why do you think the man had the photo you found at Monte Alban?"

"I nearly killed that guy, Chango."

"Yes, I know. Fortunately, you did not."

"You're telling me that after you sent me to Monte Alban on a wild goose chase, you changed your mind and sent this guy after me?"

"Yes."

"A little dramatic, wouldn't you say? Something a little less forceful than another attack might have been easier. What if he'd KO'd me and left the photo on my unconscious body? A simple phone call would have sufficed, you know."

"I didn't want you to think I was playing with you."

"Great, thanks a lot. I'm sure your messenger appreciated it, too."

"He was just a little too, how do you say, overenthusiastic. It was my people who helped you escape at Palenque, *amigo*. You didn't know that. If you weren't my friend, I wouldn't have cared."

"You were playing with my life, Chango, besides, if you knew all this, why didn't you do it yourself?"

"You were a step ahead of us. You're good at this game, my friend. You lost us there for a while after Palenque."

"We went back a long ways."

"That's why I won't kill you, Juanito. Now hand over the bloodstone."

"So, it comes down to this?"

"Please, I am serious. Hand it to me slowly."

Pastor started to hand over the treasure, but as he did several men, including Sonny Boston and José Matanza, with pistol in hand, appeared behind Chango. On either side of them, Matanza gunmen held assault rifles. Pastor quickly, and surreptitiously, slipped the bloodstone into an inside jacket of his coat.

"José, Sonny." Pastor greeted the gangsters like long lost friends. Chango spun to face the new usurpers but had no choice but to lower his own weapon. "Fellows, it's great to see you, but it's getting a little crowded around here."

"Shut up, *gringo*," one of Matanza's men said.

"Still hiring from the psych ward, *ey*, José," Pastor noted wryly.

"Still a loser, huh, Pastor." Matanza wagged his pistol. "Once a failure, always a failure. And you, Morales, drop the gun or die. Mr. Boston here doesn't like violence and we wouldn't want to upset him."

Despite the warning, Chango made an ill-advised attempt to fight back. He raised his pistol but before he could get off a round, Matanza and his two gunmen blasted away. Rounds hit Chango in the chest and leg, knocking him back against the pyramid. He slid down its side, blood staining the rocks.

"Hey, hey, stop." Pastor held up his hands. "Take it easy."

"Be careful, Mr. Pastor," Matanza advised, "or you'll end up like your corrupt friend there."

"Did you have to shoot him?" Boston sighed. "You know I don't like this sort of thing when I'm around."

"So sorry," Matanza sneered.

"This is how you plan to get your daughter back, Sonny, I mean Mr. Boston?" Pastor needled the big boss. "Kill everybody in sight?"

"*Step*daughter."

"Pardon me. *Step*daughter. Your sense of paternal love is overwhelming."

"And your mouth can get you killed, Pastor."

"By you, Sonny? I thought you were opposed to violence."

"Where's Anne? Where have you hidden her? How did you get her past us?"

"Trade secret."

"Where is she, Pastor?" Boston looked at Matanza who stepped forward and drove a hard right fist into Pastor's stomach.

"Safe," Pastor coughed and spluttered. "So that I'll be safe, too."

"You idiot," Boston growled. "I knew where you were. You both led me to the stone."

"Ah, the loving father. If you knew where we were, Sonny, you'd know where she is now. You don't know shit. Somebody else tipped you, probably poor Chango lying over there."

"What touching concern for your dying, double crossing friend," Boston snipped. "Now hear me, Pastor, I'll make this simple. Give me the bloodstone and tell me where Anne is and we all walk. You can go back to your pathetic life in Mexico City or wherever anyone is foolish enough to pay for your services. If you don't talk, you end up like your fellow loser on the ground there."

"No dice, Boston. I want out of here. Then I'll tell you where the girl is."

"Kill him," Matanza spit out, "stupid yanqui fool."

"You're really tough, huh, Matanza." Pastor's voice was full of hate. "Against women and children."

"Shut up, *cabrón*. I'll kill you just like I—"

"Stop it, José," Boston ordered. "This is your last chance, Pastor."

"Now wait a minute, Sonny, before you—"

"Enough talk." Matanza raised his pistol. "Let me kill him."

Just as Matanza tightened his finger around the pistol trigger, a woman's voice, one that Pastor immediately recognized, called out from behind the outlaws. "This is the police, drop your weapons, now. You are all under arrest."

The pronouncement was met by an explosion of gunfire from Matanza and his men, which triggered an equally rapid response from the police, who seemed to be all over the place and in force. Pastor took advantage of the noise and confusion to dive to his right, simultaneously pulling out his own pistol. Just as he did, a Matanza bullet smashed against the side of the pyramid where he had been standing.

Pastor returned two fast rounds, both of which missed the mark. In the subsequent raging firefight, the two sides found what cover they could behind large rocks and chunks of ruins. In the hail of gunfire, both of Matanza's men fell as well as one of the policemen.

Matanza and Pastor, meanwhile, were engaged in a private battle. They took turns shooting from behind hiding places. One of Matanza's shots ricocheted off the rocks behind which Pastor hid, spraying him with stinging gravel. Pastor fired off a round in retaliation, then ducked down and maneuvered around the side of the rock.

Matanza leaned out from his protection to fire again but Pastor fired two quick rounds, the first hitting rock, the second hitting Matanza squarely in the forehead. The heavy mafioso fell face first to the ground. With Claudia at the front, the police emerged to gather around the downed combatants.

"Where's Boston?" Pastor ran up to her. "What happened to Boston?"

"Forget him," Claudia said. "He can't escape."

"I'm going after him."

"John, wait. Stop."

Pastor ignored Claudia's cries and raced after Boston alone. He ran past the dead body of Matanza and toward the outer reaches of Chichen Itza where it joined the Yucatan jungle. He ran several more yards into the bush, stopped and looked around. Ahead, he saw Boston struggling to get through the heavy undergrowth. Unaccustomed as he was to the environment, Boston was an easy target and Pastor quickly caught him.

"Stop right there, Boston, or you're going to be food for tropical maggots."

Boston tried to escape but the big PI leapt forward and knocked him down. They struggled on the ground until Pastor rolled Boston over and sat on top of him where he slapped the renowned swindler several times in the face, hard. Bleeding and beaten, Boston surrendered.

"Here he is." Pastor pulled his adversary upright and drug him by the collar over to Claudia, who now also had the wounded Chango in custody. "Father of the year."

"Yes, and I'm sure his daughter will be happy to see her *papi* dearest."

"Naturally, you knew all about this crap, right, Claudia?"

"We knew a good deal."

"And I suppose you and your pals here are *Federales*?"

"I suppose you would like to see our badges?"

"The idea had occurred to me."

Claudia produced an identification badge which she handed over.

"Chief Investigator, Federal Indigenous Treasures Unit," Pastor read. "Well, what do you know, the real McCoy at last. You didn't get here a damn minute too soon, you know. I mean, you might have jumped in a little bit earlier."

"You might have trusted me and not run off from Villahermosa."

"I didn't know you were the blasted head of the *Federales* then, did I?"

"I couldn't tell you, then."

"Well, I couldn't tell you either and I was afraid Palenque would be hot, and it was. Even hotter than I expected."

"That's all past now, John. May I have the bloodstone knife, please?"

"Couldn't I keep it just a little longer?"

"It will be on display in the Museum of Anthropology."

"If I give it to you, will you promise to be my personal guide on a tour of the museum?"

"It will be my pleasure."

"Then here you go."

Pastor handed Claudia the knife. They stood facing each other, hands lightly touching.

"This will make you a hero to the Mexican people."

"Like Zapata?" Pastor suggested.

"Well, maybe not that much of a hero."

"Still, don't heroes usually get the spoils of victory? Don't they at least get the girl?"

"We are a generous people." Claudia said.

"I was counting on that."

"Maybe you've earned that vacation you wanted to take."

"They're not much fun alone."

"What about the girl?"

"She's safe in Merida. With my friend Hector's family."

"I'll send my people for her right away."

"As long as I get paid for doing the job," Pastor said, "anybody can finish it up that wants to. That should leave us both free."

"I think I might have some time off coming to me."

"And I know the perfect place." Pastor described Hector's place. "Not far from here. By the ocean. It's got sand, surf, sea—it's quiet, shady, cool."

"Sounds wonderful."

"It could be."

Claudia put her arm around Pastor's waist and when she did she noticed the bandage on his wound and the pack of cigarettes he had been carrying all the way across the country.

"You're hurt."

"Nothing to worry about. I just got grazed."

"Good. I'll make sure it's okay later. As for now you won't be needing these." Claudia took the cigarettes out of his pocket and started to toss them away. "My God, John, look."

They examined the pack together. A bullet had ripped through Pastor's shirt from a side angle, tearing a hole through the pack of cigarettes. He held it up and whistled.

"Maybe I was meant to live, after all."

"I'm sure of it." She pitched the pack to one of her men, who looked it over in amazement.

"Let's get out of here." Pastor said.

"I'm with you."

Pastor and Claudia walked away from *El Castillo* arm in arm, then, leaving her men to clean up the post-battle scene.

It was still early in the day and the tourists, most of whom had missed the deadly events that had just transpired, began to fill the archaeological site. Above them, the bright Yucatan sun shone down on the ancient ruins of Chichen Itza bathing it in a strong yellow light that emphasized its immenseness, beauty, and eternal mystery.

J.B. Hogan is a prolific and award-winning author. He grew up in Fayetteville, Arkansas, but moved to Southern California in 1961 before entering the U. S. Air Force in 1964. After the military, he went back to college, receiving a Ph.D. in English from Arizona State University in 1979.

J.B. has published over 250 stories and poems. His novels, *The Apostate, Living Behind Time, Losing Cotton*, and *Tin Hollow*—as well as his local baseball history book, *Angels in the Ozarks*, a short story collection entitled *Fallen*, and his book of poetry, *The Rubicon*—are available at Amazon, iBooks, Barnes & Noble, Books-A-Million, and Walmart.

When he's not writing or teaching, J.B. plays upright bass in East of Zion, a family band specializing in bluegrass-flavored Americana music, and is active in the Washington County (AR) Historical Society, where he's recently served as President.

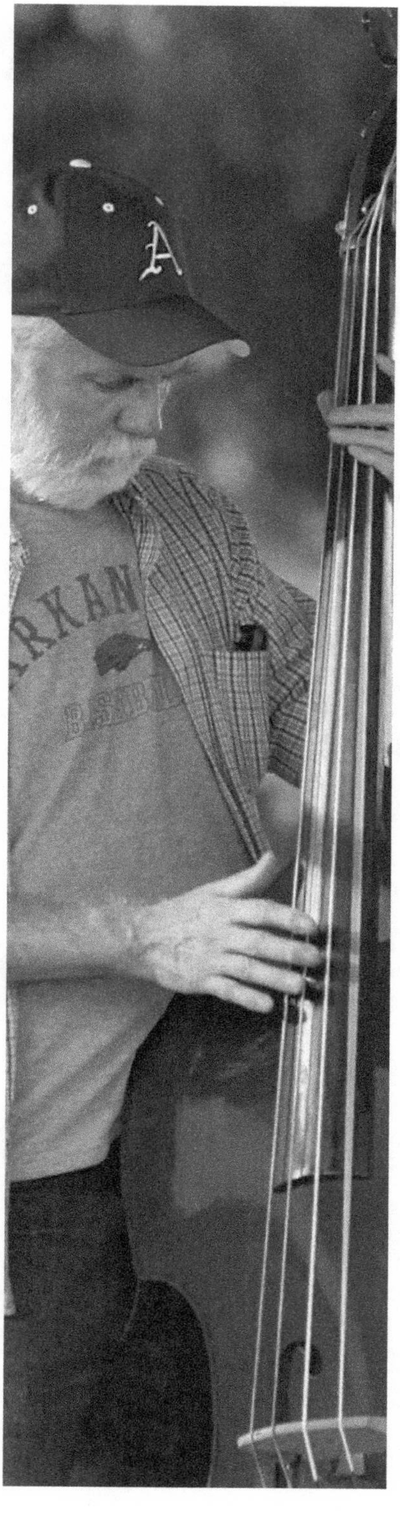

www.thejbhogan.com